Praise for *Miss Lai*

'*Miss Laila, Armed and Dangerous* is, undoubtedly, one of the most scathing social and political satires of our times. It's funny even when it makes you reel in horror, and it makes you hope even in the throes of despair. It is a book that will make you think. It is a book to slowly savour and turn in your mind long after it's over.' *The Quint*

'The plot of *Miss Laila* reads much like a thriller but with the mocking voice of political satire ... Joseph is brazen in depicting the politics of both sides as equally absurd. Bold and genuinely funny.' *Open*

'Joseph has a talent for puncturing the smug assumptions of the well-intentioned, while directing the gaze to deep injustices with a lightness of touch you wouldn't suspect... The most memorable moments are the ones between Laila and her younger sister Aisha... a throwaway moment of quiet love in an otherwise frenetic, wisecracking book, bristling with opinions and politics.' *Elle*

'Joseph's subversion of the conventions of fiction is in the same vein as Arundhati Roy's *The Ministry of Utmost Happiness*, in which readers get an extensive insight into the author's musings on where our culture is headed.' *The Hindu*

'Joseph's *Miss Laila Armed and Dangerous* further establishes him as one of most engaging storytellers and insightful interpreters of our times. With the rigour of lean and unsentimental prose, the novel weaves a gripping tale set in contemporary India and echoes all the key whispers and screams that mark country's conversations with itself... [When] VS Naipaul said that novels had outlived their utility and were likely to be replaced by cinema as a powerful form of storytelling, he perhaps didn't anticipate writers like Manu Joseph, who can illuminate both worlds.' *News Laundry*

'A compulsive read, Joseph's often clever, sometimes wise and always entertaining new novel combines elements of satire and the political thriller.' *India Today*

'Wicked, sarcastic and garnished with wit. Some readers will laugh, raise eyebrows and even disagree with portions of this novel, but this is certainly not a book to be missed.' *The Book Satchel*

Praise for *Serious Men*

'The finest comic novelists know that a small world can illuminate a culture and an age. With this funny-sad debut, Joseph does just that for surging, fractious India ... The absurdity and humiliation of social exclusion drives the comedy of one of the year's most auspicious debuts ...' Boyd Tonkin, *The Independent*

'Manu Joseph's satirical tale of an ostensibly new India still in thrall to its caste-ridden and sexist traditions is so much more than a mere comic caper.' Catherine Taylor, *The Guardian*

'Manu Joseph, a leading journalist in India, has written a debut novel that skewers a society where new ambitions and older class divisions co-exist. From the contrasts of contemporary India, he extracts pointed, often bitter comedy.' *The Sunday Times*

'This is arguably the best of the recent crop of novels by Indian writers ... it does for India in the age of globalization what Salman Rushdie and Rohinton Mistry did for earlier eras ... If there is one novel you must buy this year, make it this one ...' Anis Shivani, *Huffington Post*

'*Serious Men* could well be the most exciting debut in Indian writing in English since Arundhati Roy's *The God of Small Things*.'
Usha K.R., *Deccan Herald*

'I've been meaning to read one of Manu Joseph's novels since I heard him speak at a literary festival a couple of years ago. His comments had a witty arrogance and a weirdness that I thought augured well for his prose. And I was right! *Serious Men*, published in 2010, is the funniest, most stylish book I've read this year.'

Zoe Heller, Best Books of 2014, *New York Times*

'Joseph is an acute, sensitive observer and his writing accumulates the myriad circumstantial details of everyday life which makes it real ... It's been a very good year for South Asian English novels and *Serious Men* could be the pick of the crop.' Pratik Kanjilal, *Hindustan Times*

'Manu Joseph's triumph is ... in creating characters whom it's impossible not to care about, in a plot which it's impossible not to enjoy.'

Anita Roy, *Outlook*

'Manu Joseph's debut *Serious Men* merits a one-word review: Hurrah! For here at last is a novel that keeps its wits, is nimble on its feet and speaks its informed mind in stylish prose ... It is replete with wit and barbed with anger that unerringly finds its mark. '

Kalpish Ratna, *Tehelka (Weekly)*

Praise for *The Illicit Happiness of Other People*

'Joseph writes with extraordinary wit, cunning and sympathy about both family relationships and ultimate mysteries.'

Starred Review, *Kirkus Reviews*

'Joseph's smart new novel is laced with black humour and keen observations on human nature ... Joseph's rich characters intersect in moments of tenderness, yet each continues along a path that gracefully highlights the titular Other and the emotional divides that separate individuals. Lucky for us, Joseph's empathic prose deftly bridges those gaps.' *Publishers Weekly*

'Manu Joseph's prose is clear, wry, dry and witty – reminiscent of the work of Haruki Murakami.' Ariel Balter, *New York Journal of Books*

'*The Illicit Happiness of Other People* is ambitious ... It is a plot-driven yarn with themes of morality, sexuality, psychiatry and yet more science and philosophy ... but it does not feel overburdened ... quite an achievement.' *The Economist*

'Both wittily funny and darkly serious.' Harry Ritchie, *Daily Mail*

'Joseph twists what I feared would be a book for people wanting a second *White Tiger* into a cocktail of character, culture and religion ... Joseph's prose is exquisitely phrased without an excess of sentimentality ... the confident, immersing voice promises readers this is not the last we've heard of Manu Joseph.' Christine Edwall, *The Telegraph*

'A stylishly written book, which starts out as being darkly comical, and then grows progressively darker and more disturbing.'
Anvar Alikhan, *India Today*

Miss Laila, Armed and Dangerous

MISS LAILA, ARMED AND DANGEROUS

MANU JOSEPH

First published in the UK 2018 by
Myriad Editions
An imprint of New Internationalist Publications
The Old Music Hall, 106–108 Cowley Rd
Oxford OX4 1JE

www.myriadeditions.com

First printing
1 3 5 7 9 10 8 6 4 2

Originally published in India by Fourth Estate
An imprint of HarperCollins Publishers India

A CIP catalogue record for this book
is available from the British Library

ISBN (pbk): 978-1-912408-10-8
ISBN (ebk): 978-1-912408-11-5

Designed in Arno Pro at Sürya, New Delhi

Printed and bound in Great Britain
by Clays Ltd, St Ives plc

MANU JOSEPH is the author of two previous widely acclaimed and bestselling novels, *Serious Men* (winner of the Hindu Literary Prize and the PEN/Open Book Award) and *The Illicit Happiness of Other People* (shortlisted for the Encore Award and the Hindu Literature Prize). A former columnist for the *International New York Times,* he lives in Delhi and writes for *Mint Lounge.*

1

Around 7:30 a.m.

WHEN SHE RETURNS from a long run she finds her neighbours standing almost naked in the compound. Men in morose Y-front underwear, women crouched behind parked cars or hidden inside rings formed by other women who are not bare. Through the gaps in the cordons she sees flashes of naked thighs, waists, backs. It is Friday but that does not explain anything.

Akhila, in damp shorts and vests and a blue bandana, does not stop to find out what has happened. She is confident of solving the puzzle any moment. Everything that happens in Mumbai has happened before. She walks across the concrete driveway towards Beach Towers even though the behaviour of the residents should have warned her against entering the twenty-storey building.

The possibility of death does not occur to her. It never does. If she is ever in an air crash, she knows, she would be that lone miraculous survivor. She might even save a child. It is not hope, which is merely a conversation with the self. Hope is a premonition of defeat. She knew that even as a little girl who used to wait for her mother to return, wait for days, for weeks. Optimism, on the other hand, is psychosis. Its victims alone know how cheerfully the disease takes them to doom. She has tried but is unable to have complete faith in the view that she will die one day. Science will find a way to make her immortal.

People find immortality amusing because they do not believe they deserve it. Like a gorgeous spouse. But death is merely a technology of the universe, and a time comes, doesn't it, when a science becomes obsolete.

Apart from immortality she has no grand suspicions about her life. It will be filled with friends, solitary sometimes, and beautiful, of course, as it is for people who run long distances. There might even be greatness at some point, but she is not very clear about the details.

She sprints up the stairs to the ninth floor as she usually does. She is still on the first flight of stairs when she hears the lift doors open. It should have been an unremarkable event, but this morning the doors have a loud clear voice and there are echoes. Echoes are rare in Mumbai.

From the lift emerges a tiny ancient woman with a mild hunch, her forearms splayed, holding in each hand a pressed kurta folded on a hanger. The old woman, in a lovely cotton sari, moves at an excruciating pace but manages to get out of the lift a moment before the closing doors can crush her. And she appears to know where she is going with the two hangers. Akhila follows her but it is hard to stay behind; the woman is too slow. It is as though she is lampooning the senior, which is not beyond her, actually. She watches the old woman walk out into the driveway, towards a ring of women guarding the nudes. There, a man has begun to undress, looking valiant in his late decision. He flings his shirt first, then his trousers into the ring of women.

Akhila turns back and runs up the stairs in the unfamiliar silence of vacant homes. The stairway is littered with objects, which is unusual. There are pieces of clothing, eerie dolls, one daft Nokia that surely belongs to a maid, even food. There are footwear, and a streak of blood too. So much happens when people flee.

At home, she does the usual stretches on the balcony, watching the Arabian Sea. The sky is a clear blue. Far away a giant cruise ship sails across the bay, like a beautiful novel about nothing. A hectic breeze arrives. The winding bridge over the sea stands like a marvel. Her father hates that bridge. He complains about it every day to her, but she is spared this morning because he is not in town. Something about majestic cable-stayed bridges across shallow seas remind Marxists that they have lost to capitalism and human nature.

She walks to the kitchen, checking her phone, but there are messages that make her stop. They ask if she is alright. Several messages uniformly ask the question, 'Did you feel it?' When she sees the Twitter feed she figures that about half an hour ago there were tremors. That explains the neighbours. But the thought of fleeing the building still does not occur to her.

The tremors were mild, but an eighty-year-old, condemned building in Prabhadevi has collapsed. She is drawn to the images of the fallen building. She knows the place, it is not far. There are people still trapped in its debris.

In minutes, she is sprinting down, her spiral curls flailing. She has showered and changed into jeans and a T-shirt that has no message at all to convey.

She runs out of Beach Towers, through a mob of neighbours who are beginning to feel foolish. 'She even had a bath,' a woman mutters.

Akhila wonders why they had not stopped her from going up. They may not like her, or they probably thought she knew what she was doing, but still they should have tried to stop her. She likes the idea of a village of people, even if they are nude, asking her to be one of them.

2

A Patriarch's Review

SHE DOES NOT offend him. To be infuriated by a young woman is to accept that the world is an unfamiliar place. But he cannot assure her that the other patriots, the young especially, who are performing their morning drills outside on the bald grounds of the shakha, marching, kicking, screaming, swinging their sticks and swords, have such a view of life. They are susceptible to offence.

The bachelors look serious in the sacred attire – the tilted black cap, white shirt, sleeves folded at the elbows, large billowing khaki shorts with pleats. Just the sight of Hindu patriots this way in the uniform of the Sangh reminds Muslims of death, and infuriates the refined cultural orphans who have been retarded by English. Even to Professor Vaid's old eyes they look intimidating. That is the idea. Hinduism without fear and wound is probably called Buddhism.

Vaid, too, is in uniform. So is the young patriot on whose arms the laptop rests. The girl in the computer, too, but she is wearing red shoes that have long pointed heels. No one has ever seen a woman in these clothes. Her name, she says, is

Akhila Iyer. The young patriot finally places the laptop on the desk, which the excessively pious simpleton should have done much earlier. The problem with reverence in this country is that some people convert it into a folk dance.

In Miss Iyer's film, which has gone viral after it was uploaded last night, she stands against a dark background and talks to an unseen audience. She pulls at the hems of her enormous shorts and says, in English, 'The most dangerous men in my country wear divided skirts.'

There is no such thing as courage. There is gamble, yes. And there is ignorance. Miss Iyer probably imagines violence as a journalistic event, something that happens in another place to another kind of people. Many make that mistake. Their corpses, they look so surprised. Bewildered corpses that wear one footwear on one lifeless foot, he has seen them many times. He has never understood the asymmetries of the dead. Where does the other shoe go?

Miss Iyer has large eyes set in a clever Aryan face, her wiry hair dense and wild. She is probably not even twenty-five, she is at least five decades younger than him. A long-forgotten thought comes to him, that there is something precarious about the life of an attractive woman.

In her film, which is called *White Beard*, Miss Akhila Iyer claims that she is the first woman ever to be granted admission to the Sangh. She says she had sent her milkman to pay twenty rupees at the local shakha and bought a membership. She waves the receipt in the air. 'There must be a more proper way for a lady to join Hindu nationalism,' she says. 'It's the twenty-first century, guys, why can't they let women join the gang?

I tell you I totally qualify. A) I am unmarried. B) There is a badass cultural guardian in me. C) For the past several weeks I've been celibate too.'

'What is the meaning of badass?' Vaid asks.

There is silence in the room. The boys probably imagine that a man of his stature should not be told. Or, maybe they do not know the meaning. Nashik is a small town.

Miss Iyer says, 'I kind of like being an Indian Nazi.' And she gives a Nazi salute, which is a deliberate misrepresentation. The Hindu patriots were, of course, inspired by the Nazis but they have their own salute, which she now does correctly.

The camera is still and never shows her audience, but they surely exist in the darkened room, which is probably a bar. From the laughter, which is occasional, and her gaze that sweeps but does not rise above a certain degree, he presumes her audience is small. Also, it would be impossible for her to perform the act in front of more than a hundred people. Beyond that many people, anywhere in the nation, there would be at least two nationalists who would be seriously enraged and one of them would be rich enough to afford to fling a shoe at her.

She says that she is going to tell a story. 'Stories are all we have,' she says. 'Everything we believe in. Everything we think about. They are stories, they come from stories. Then there is masturbation. We love it not only because it is about sex. Masturbation is, primarily, a story.'

Surely, she speaks for women alone?

It is not clear at this point why she needs to be in the costume of the Sangh. She is probably coming to that, she is setting up a joke, perhaps about the sex lives of the patriots. Any moment now she might say something about their secret homosexuality. That would be another old lazy joke. He throws a glance at the steady stream of patriots trickling into his office after the morning drill, their thin legs hairy, bare thighs paltry, some paunches so enormous that they stun the belt buckles. Only women would agree to sleep with them.

On the sleek television that is mounted on the saffron wall, studio analysts have started their chat, but the volume is on mute. Soon the Election Commission will begin declaring the results. The ejaculations of the Nehru–Gandhi dynasty will be flushed, and the suave imitators of the West will be shown their place as mere foreigners in their own land. The political masquerade of the Sangh will triumph. The controls of the ancient nation will pass from dynasty to monastery.

'In *Fifty Shades of Grey*,' says Miss Iyer, and waits for the giggles to dissolve. 'In *Fifty Shades of Grey*, a telecom billionaire spanks a humanities student who believes that the internet has to be fair and free.' Miss Iyer takes a slow sip of water from a small bottle that she is holding. 'He has a written contract for her to sign, which would give him the right to spank her. She asks two important questions. Can she, too, spank him? He says, "No." She does not press. And she asks, despite her suspicion that she might enjoy the spanking, as some of you do, what she would get in return for being spanked. The billionaire says, "Me." This, we know, is the treaty in all loyal relationships where the whips and chains may not usually appear to be whips and chains. Men and women let themselves be bound, held in captivity and abused to a permissible degree on the promise that in return they would get the other.'

For all her charade, Miss Iyer is not a comedian. He can see that much. She is something else, something more political.

'Sorry, I got a bit serious,' she says, defending what she is in reality. Serious. Like comedians overplay their serious sides in their real lives, the serious often try to be amusing when they perform to an audience. That is why the world looks so awkward.

'What I really want to say is my boyfriend left me last month,' she says. Her audience lets out sounds of sophisticated empathy. 'We had been together for two years. One Saturday evening last month, when we were watching a film about baboons on YouTube, he told me he was leaving me. There was no warning. "I love you too much," he said. "And you're always about to get into trouble. Never understood why you're so reckless. I can't sleep any more. I keep thinking something bad is going to happen to you. I can't take it any more." Which is all sweet, you know, but he also said, and that I think was the real issue, he wanted to "be free". He found me suffocating, which I am.

'But, my delicious yogi, you downward-facing dog, what did you expect? An easy love? This is how it works, sweetheart, to be in love is to agree to bondage.

'Come back, my love. Let's make up, twice, as usual, and faff for hours in the spoon position.

'I suppose the point I'm trying to make here is that it looks like I am single again. And, you know what, strangely, the past few weeks I've been thinking a lot about Damodarbhai.'

On the dark background, which is probably a curtain, the image of 'Damodarbhai' appears. The son of the Sangh, the chosen one, the face that has been appointed by the patriarchs to be the mask. He is in a Nehru jacket, which needs to be renamed; his full white beard groomed and oiled, eyes shrewd, lips glistening, his grey hair more abundant than Vaid remembers. He is one of those men who suspect they are handsome. The past twelve years, since the slaughter of Muslims in Gujarat, he has been ascending across the nation. The liberals have been trying to send him to prison. They got the United States to ban his entry for crimes against humanity. But there is no evidence that indicts him, except one. Hindus adore him and they cannot explain why.

There is a grunt of a young man standing near the Patriarch. The unhappy patriot clenches his fists. 'If she says anything about him, about our prince, if she says anything nasty about our future prime minister, I won't spare her.' The other patriots, too, look angry.

But Miss Iyer's audience boos Damodarbhai. She asks people to calm down. When silence returns, she points to the image behind her and says, 'Look at this man. There is a reason why some people call him India's Putin. Look at this man-man. He is the exact opposite of my father. When my dad walks into a room, he knows nobody wants to sleep with him. Just look at him. How tragic for women that he has chosen to be celibate. He says he has always been celibate. How weird, between the Pope and Damodarbhai, two virgins rule half the world.

'This is a man who knows he is extraordinary and life is merely a slow confirmation. If a smart soldier were to go up to him and whisper, "Chief, I am from the future. The machines have taken over the world and you are mankind's last stand. You sent me back in time on a mission," Damodarbhai would totally believe him.

'And I don't really think he is as evil as people make him out to be. I don't believe he is India's most dangerous man. He did not ask a mob of Hindus to slaughter Muslims. Damodarbhai did not send the thugs who massacred and hacked and raped, and burnt children alive. There is not a shred of evidence. Hundreds of millions of Hindus know that. That's why they worship him. Because he is innocent.'

In sarcasm one says the exact opposite of what one means. It is the second-lowest form of humour, it is too easy. Through such low devices, though, she rebukes a nation that has fallen in love with Damodarbhai. Is she then one of them? Yet another young woman who, like the State, is the actuality of an ethical idea?

Her website says that she is a student of neurosurgery who has taken a one-year break before she heads to Johns Hopkins. Usually, science students do not become gadflies. Including women, despite their wounds, so many wounds. They have too much to study, and too much at stake in the present and in the future. And they are not trained in lament as students of liberal arts are. Science students are drawn to the strong. He himself was a student of physics when he joined the Sangh. Decades later, when he was chosen to lead the great organization, he was a nuclear scientist. That was a long time ago, when he was in his fifties, the infancy of old age. He has since relinquished all administrative powers. He is now just another old man in the Sangh.

'The Sangh has returned. The Hindu Reich is coming,' Miss Iyer says in theatrical glee. 'Damodarbhai is here, bow to Lord Voldemort. Everyone has to choose a side.'

The Patriarch is grateful that the secular intellectual dig this time was derived from Harry Potter. Usually, it is *Animal Farm*.

Something about her reminds him of people who are not quite what they seem. He sits at his desk and explores her website. It turns out Miss Iyer has gained some notoriety as a performer. Sometimes, as she does in *White Beard*, she talks to small gatherings, which she claims is 'Stand-up Anthropology'. How abused the idea of 'anthropology' is. People wish to be amusing, yet they want to be called anthropologists.

Her films are not all monologues. Most of her films, in fact, are pranks. That is where she gets confusing. She never pranks the patriots. Most of her victims are liberal eggheads.

'Professor,' a young patriot says. He is trying hard to be respectful but is unable to hide his excitement. 'My friends called from Mumbai. An old building has collapsed.'

The boy now seethes.

'This girl, she is there.'

3

Around 8:00 a.m.

THE CARS PARKED on the narrow lane have begun to nod in the surge of jostling men who have come to see the fallen building. Akhila is stranded in the mob, about fifty metres away from the site. There are only men all around her. She considers walking along the edge of the street so that she can climb a tree or a wall if trouble begins, but there is no guarantee the approach would be any safer. There are men on the walls, too, and they stand as though in queue. Behind the walls that flank the lane, in the tall residential buildings, whole families have gathered in their little balconies, looking in one direction, sipping hot drinks, combing hair, talking on their cell phones. The ones on the higher floors can probably see the rubble.

Every passing moment there are more men pouring into the lane. It is probably a very bad idea for her to be here. Some characters are taking a good look at her even as they are pressing ahead. She transfers her backpack, which contains emergency medicines, to her front, appointing the bag yet again the armour of her breasts.

She wishes J were with her. He would not have come on his own, she would have had to drag him along as she normally did to take him anywhere. He is still her background hum. Come back, honeybunch, come back to your woman and do your mussing and kissing, and be the witness, as you once were, to her days. How long before she solves this ache, which is chiefly in her temples and throat. Is that where love hurts for athletes with fabulous resting heart rates. And if the ache never leaves, would she become one of those girls who post on Facebook the sad obituary of their love, 'Stranger, Friend, Lover, Friend, Stranger'. And would she, too, remain unhappy into her late twenties, wasting her best years in the memory of a mere adorable boy.

There is a commotion on the street, and the mob begins to flee. The men on the walls leap down and sprint. A dozen cops appear at the rear of the fleeing crowd, waving their sticks and slamming them on asses and lower limbs. It is astonishing how fast Indian men can run when they are inspired.

She stays. She stands pretending to talk on her cell phone, a careful denial of danger that usually disorientates aggressive stray dogs. The men run past her. The cops, too, ignore her. The lane is clear just like that.

She walks towards the knot of fire engines, ambulances and television OB vans. She knows the street well but not the fallen building. The entrance to its compound is narrow, about as wide as a large car, where there are a dozen cops. It appears that entry is restricted. The building never had a gate, so the traffic police has erected a barricade. She can see the dwarf mountain of debris, about twenty feet high. There are swarms of firemen and civilians on the debris, shovelling. Near the barricade there is a tight group of reporters and photographers. There are probably not many of them about. It is unlikely the building collapse will even feature on any of the channels. All news is going to be about Damodarbhai. Also, the fallen building was a low-income kind of place.

She stands with the journalists in the hope that they might smuggle her in. The photographers have worn their beige sleeveless vests that make them look capable. Their poise and banter appear to have subdued the reporters who are with them. It is this way with calamities – the photographers have all the shine. Nobody is talking about Damodarbhai or the election results. At least not yet.

A large man who is carrying a tripod on his shoulder is in the middle of narrating a story, which is about a telephone call that a government clerk in Delhi made to his mother who was in the doomed building. She is probably still in there. The source of the information, according to the narrator, was the clerk himself. He had called his mother a minute before the building fell. The mother was telling him how expensive vegetables are these days. Then the conversation changed course.

'I am feeling giddy, son.'

'Maa, are you alright?'

'I think something is happening, son.'

'Maa?'

'The plates in the kitchen are all falling down.'

'Maa.'

'The portrait of your grandfather has fallen…'

'Maa.'

'Your father has just fallen ... He is rolling towards me.'

And the line went dead, according to the narrator.

Nobody laughs, so the narrator tapers off with, 'One moment people are going about their lives. The next moment ... boom. So sad.'

Akhila feels sorry for people whose anecdotes flop. So she lets out a faint chuckle. As it happens every time she does something inappropriate, she sees in her mind the grimace of conscientious citizens whom she always imagines to be indignant women with short legs.

THIRTEEN BODIES LIE on the corridor. Six men, four women and three children, all boys. Their eyes are open in a final dejection, some look surprised. They are covered in white dust but there is very little damage to their bodies. In fact, they are entirely unscathed, their faces especially. How must they have died? Do they have huge gashes on the backs of their skulls? They await transport to the morgue to join the other corpses who have already arrived. There are no mourners, no wails in the air. That is what is eerie. Are their families dead too, or buried inside the rubble? Or, maybe they have survived and are in good care in a hospital not far away. All Akhila can hear is the sound of drills and shovels, and of men yelling in a language that appears to have been invented this morning.

The AFD Chawl is an L-shaped three-storeyed tenement the colour of pus. It runs along two sides of an almost rectangular mud plot. The other two sides of the plot are circumscribed by the wall of an adjacent building and the rear of a high-rise. Between the wall and the high-rise is the narrow entrance to the compound from where she had infiltrated the police barricade by merging with a group of television journalists. One wing of the building has completely collapsed. The other wing is intact, its broad ground-floor corridor serving as a temporary shelter for the dead recovered from the debris. There is fear that this portion of the chawl, too, will sink in but the residents have demanded that firemen not leave the dead on the open plot in full view of hundreds of spectators who have assembled in the surrounding buildings.

There are about a hundred people inside the compound, most of them residents or relatives and friends of people who are still trapped in the debris. Some of the survivors have fresh bandages on their bodies. Many of them are lined along the wall and they look more damaged than the dead.

On the debris mound, as firemen and residents dig with machines and rods, fights break out between them.

Usually, quarrels employ efficient language and those involved appear fluent and proficient, even clever, because quarrels are repetitions of fights people have had in similar circumstances. They know what to expect, so what to say, and to say it better than they did the last time. But the fights here on the debris are hollow and incoherent because the men are in unprecedented circumstances, so their arguments too have no precedence. They have to invent new insults.

'You are so fat, how can you call yourself a fireman,' a resident says in Marathi. It is true. The fireman is a bit large. Most of the firemen on the debris have enormous paunches.

That is how they have always been. Almost every day, on her way back from Worli Sea Face, as she passed by the Prabhadevi Fire Station, she has seen their daily drills. But they can do things men of their shape are not expected to – they can even climb poles, and only slightly slower than monkeys.

It is not surprising that the residents are overwhelmed by the novelty of the situation, but it is odd to see the firemen so dazed. They do not seem to have ever stood on the debris of a building. They look awkward. The residents complain that the firemen are too slow but nobody knows what exactly they must do. Where must they dig, and where must they dig fast?

Cops keep an eye on the compound wall because dozens of spectators have been trying to scale them. Huge crowds have gathered again on the narrow lane outside the society. Journalists who arrived late have begun to complain on Twitter that the cops are not letting them in.

Around the police barricades, there is a fresh altercation. Four men are arguing with the cops over something. They look tough, and all of them have a dash of red tilak on their foreheads. They look like patriots of some order and the cops are not too aggressive with them. Finally, they let the men enter. The four walk in and do not cast a glance at the debris. They appear to be looking for someone. When they see her, their eyes rest on her. She feels a stab of terror, she walks away towards a huddle of people.

Television journalists have begun their interviews. The people are easy to talk to. They talk about the mysterious rumble that lasted several seconds before the building fell and how they fled, and about the bodies scattered all over the debris. 'You can hear them,' one man says. 'There are places where if you stand long enough you can hear them. Men, women and children buried inside begging to be saved. They go quiet for some time. Then, all of a sudden, they beg again as if they have risen from sleep.'

She has not set foot on the debris yet because she is unable to resolve an issue – if she were to stand on the rubble, would she be adding to the weight that is already bearing down on the buried? It is not a trivial question, she is sure of that.

There is some activity around a portion of the debris. Photographers and cameramen and onlookers rush to the spot and a crowd grows. Standing on the ruins, his legs on uneven stones, a powerful bare young man is pulling down a rope that has been fixed on a pulley. The pulley has been tied high on the beam of a freestanding shaft. It is as though the man is drawing a huge pail of water from deep earth, but what emerges from the debris is the body of a suspended woman in a purple sari, her long black hair blowing in the wind. Strung by her shoulders, she rises with every mighty heave of the young man, who now begins to cry. He stops to watch her as she twirls above the ruins.

THE SPECTATORS WANT to believe that the death toll is high. They reveal the wish through guesses made in sombre tones. They claim to hope that most of the residents of the doomed wing had managed to flee, but they point out why that is unlikely. There was not enough time, and it was early in the morning when most of the residents were probably asleep.

According to Akhila's estimates, not more than two hundred people lived in the collapsed wing, but some of the guesses of the death toll that people make are as high as five hundred. She is repulsed, but only for a moment, because when she is repulsed she feels like Noam Chomsky. She has trained herself to make the unnatural assumption – what if the world is as humane and moral as you, what explains the action of a set of people? True though that if everyone is inclined to make such an assumption it would pretty much destroy Facebook. Maybe people do not wish anyone dead, but want the number of the dead in a calamity to be high. A remarkable number but a believable number that is not divisible by five or ten.

She hears a violent sound behind her but before she can turn she feels a sharp pain in her lower back and the air leave her lungs. The next moment she is on the ground. She is then lifted by her hair. She is facing the four men who had barged into the compound after arguing with the cops. 'Can you tell us a joke,' one of them says. They punch her, slap her. One man kicks as though that is his speciality. She catches a glimpse of one of them recording the assault on his phone. The crowd does not react. The firemen and cops don't move. She begins to fight back, bites the ear of a thug, but they throw her away with ease.

4

A Patriarch's Review

'REAL COUPLES' ARE a demographic that exists only in pornography. Their amateur home-sex videos remind the world that unattractive people too have sex. Ideally, the fact should not need reminding of. But in public imagination, including the imagination of Professor Vaid who is shaving at the moment, fornicating strangers are usually beautiful people. The source of the fallacy is part fantasy but he suspects it is chiefly professional pornography, which is a farce. What is real is the home-sex video. In such a film, unremarkable couples make love in banal ways and the woman never attains orgasm, which is a form of sound. But their sex, revealed to the world because of some treachery, is exciting – but not to Vaid any more. Their sex is exciting to most people because what they are watching is a fact.

He studies his antique nudity in the mirror. The body is slim and can stand on its head for ten minutes, yet it is hideous somehow. The only deformity of age the body has avoided is in the scalp, which is filled with short sturdy silver hair. His nose has been growing every day, it is now a massive pockmarked asteroid. He wishes there were a video from his youth, not a sex film but of him fully nude, in all his glory, doing something respectable, like watering a plant maybe or performing shirshasana. He asks if he would be devastated if his nude film went public today. Surprisingly, the question does not have a clear answer. The old bastard, too, wants glory.

The creature in the mirror has always been a lonely person, like other old bachelors. Do the lonely deserve sympathy? Some, surely, but most people are lonely because they, too, have rejected people; they have rejected lovers and friends who wished to be with them but were not good enough.

His mind has once again drifted too far from the performing art of Miss Akhila Iyer. What he was arriving at was that her pranks are not farces precisely because they are pranks. A prank is closer to anthropology than a novel and many other things that claim to be.

Miss Iyer's short film *How Feminist Men Have Sex* opens with the girl walking down a corridor of a hotel. The camera trails her as it often does in her films. She is in a white shirt and red pants, which surely have a more specific description, and comfortable blue shoes. She stops at a shut door and turns towards the camera.

'We're about to meet a top political economist. He even knows what it means. He is from Delhi. As you know, he is also a columnist, television commentator, and a man with a moral compass,' she says with a deadpan face. This is not the deadpan of a comedian whose seriousness is a part of the act and a foreboding of an approaching joke. The deadpan of Miss Iyer is not frivolous.

'Last week he published a thoughtful piece titled "Breakfast to Bed: Why Indian Men Should Be Feminists",' she goes on about the man with the moral compass, standing at the door of his hotel room. 'The essay has been read online by over a million people, including men.'

Moments after she rings the doorbell, an elegant middle-aged man opens the door. Gautam Rajan is of a type: high caste, socialist, bearded, alumnus of an American college, champion of equality, beneficiary of inequality, allergic to capitalism, large dams and nationalism. He has called Damodarbhai a 'fascist'. He probably meant it in a bad way.

Rajan is highly articulate, verbally articulate, a quality that people do not see as charlatan. But the fact is life is complex and mysterious, histories unreliable, all philosophies ambiguous, almost nothing is fully known or understood; can an honest mind ever be articulate?

Rajan is unaware that the recording has begun. Also, he is certainly not familiar with the nature of Miss Iyer's films or what the young woman is about. She walks into the hotel room and introduces the unseen cameraperson, who is a woman.

'Akhila,' Rajan says with a gracious hand on her slender shoulder, 'how nice to meet you, and how interesting to be you. And how lucky for Indian journalism that bright girls like you from science are flocking to it.'

Miss Iyer gives him a shy smile, lampooning feminine submission. 'I know I must crack a self-deprecatory joke right now, sir, but I can't think of one,' she says. It is an omen but Rajan misses it.

She probably shot the film before she began uploading her works. She probably shot most of her short films before she released any of them so that her subjects would not be forewarned.

Miss Iyer and Rajan are now seated across a coffee table.

'Start?' he says with a sideways glance at the camera, which makes him look foolish already.

'Yes, Mr Rajan.'

'Please call me Gatz.'

'Call you what?'

'Gatz.'

His phone rings. He apologizes, considers the device and kills the call.

'I see you've a Blackberry,' she says.

'Yes. I like Blackberry. I'm not an Apple fan.'

'I used to have a Blackberry, sir.'

'Everyone did, once.'

'I had a problem with its keypad. The buttons were so small. Fiddling with it was exactly like searching for my G-spot.'

Rajan issues a cautious smile, but he is yet to suspect the nature of the interview. His phone rings again, and once again he cuts the call. 'I've been on phone all day talking to journalists,' he says. 'It's unusual for me to speak as a feminist. But that's good, that's very good.'

'The journalists are still calling you about your article?'

'No, no. You've not heard the news?'

'I'm clueless, Mr Rajan.'

He says an incident occurred in the morning. A professor of creative writing has caused a major stir. 'This jerk said during a panel discussion that he has to just read a short-story submission without knowing who the author is and he would be able to tell if the writer is a woman. Don't these guys ever stop? How many imbeciles are there in the academic and literary world?'

'Did he say, Mr Rajan, what makes him identify a female writer so easily?'

Rajan is surprised by the question. 'No. These guys are never that specific.'

'Maybe what he meant was that when a short story is deep and brilliant and without gimmicks the author is usually a woman.'

'That's not what he meant, I am sure.'

'The fact, Mr Rajan, that he can identify the author of a work as a woman also means, by default, he can tell if the author is a man. Why aren't men pissed?'

Rajan throws a quick look at the camera. 'My dear girl,' he says, 'his statement has a specific meaning. There is a context to it. And there is history. There is a tacit insult in this sort of view. And every woman knows what he means.'

'Every woman?'

'Every woman.'

'Three billion women must be a single collective organism.'

His face grows serious, he throws another nervous look at the camera. A gentle smile of incomprehension appears on his face. She stares at him in silence as though expecting him to say more. When he is about to speak and end the bizarre silence, she interrupts him with a question. 'Mr Rajan, what do you mean when you say you are a feminist?'

He takes a moment. And when he speaks he stresses every syllable. 'Equality.' He then repeats it more emphatically, 'Equality. Unambiguous non-negotiable equality.'

'Equal to whom? Equal to men? Equal to you? But there must be more to a woman's life.'

Rajan tries to achieve a graceful nod.

'Equality and respect,' he says. 'Unambiguous non-negotiable respect. When men respect women they are feminists.'

'Can they watch pole-dancing?'

'Excuse me?'

'Is a male feminist allowed to watch pole-dancing?'

Rajan rubs his nose. 'Informed, intelligent men do not objectify women.'

'Have you, sir, ever objectified a woman?'

'This is the dumbest question in the world.'

'It's the dumbest question in the world because you obviously do objectify women?'

'I never. Never. Never.'

'How do you fuck?'

Rajan begins a long glare at the camera. He is not sure yet whether this is a prank. If the interview is genuine and he terminates it, he would look petty, like sensitive Hindu patriots whom he condemns. He is a liberal, and liberals must stay the course of an unpleasant interview. He shifts his stare to Miss Iyer. His paunch begins to rise and fall with every deep breath. 'I don't do that...'

'You don't bonk?'

'First of all it's called "making love".'

'Making love.'

'Yes, making love.'

'Do you, sir, make love?'

'I am the kind of man who gets excited by a woman's intellect, spirit and humour.'

'As in your lady is sitting on the bed reading and you look at her and think, "Oh my adorable lady devouring Roger Penrose." And you are consumed by an intense respect for her, which makes you very, very hard.'

Miss Iyer shuts her eyes and begins to pant. 'In the yellow light of the Japanese lampshade that you bought because she was busy, as you see her middle-aged face and sagging neck, you ogle at her deep inner intelligence and wit, and your respect is escalating, and now you're so hard it's hurting you.'

Rajan says in a low, shivering voice, 'What's going on?'

Miss Iyer rises but her eyes are still shut and she is panting harder. She holds an imaginary body and begins gentle pelvic movements that suggest, in Vaid's biased perception, doggy sex. '"Darling … darling … I so respect you … Tell me something cleverly funny; tell me once again, darling, why did you read Hegelian dialectics upside down." And your darling moans, "Because, Baby, as a Marxist that's the only way I can read Hegel right." You're in a tizzy now, sir, she is so clever. You're so, so hard.'

Rajan turns to the camera, which moves back a few feet. 'Leave,' he says.

But Miss Iyer goes on, continuing her pelvic action: 'You say, "Darling, let's move on to general knowledge. What's the most common name in Vietnam?" And she says, with a perfect Vietnamese accent, while somehow managing to moan, "Nguyen, Nguyen." You, sir, rasp, "I respect you so ... darling. Next quiz question, honey. What's the difference between recursion and iteration?"'

Rajan rises. A bird-like sound leaves his lungs.

'Sir,' Miss Iyer says, 'I don't follow your dialect any more.'

A PRANK NEED not have an objective, but Miss Iyer does. The messages in *How Feminist Men Have Sex* are simple: the impossibility of sex as a reverential act, and that modern men who claim to be feminists without the experience of living in a female body are frauds; and that an erection is the same hydraulic event in political economists as it is in jackasses.

But Miss Iyer probably has a deeper objective.

Taken together, her many pranks reveal a pattern. Her victims are rich Marxists, socialists, environmentalists, actually anyone in this country who eats salad; also agitators against large dams; foes of genetically modified organisms; summer interns from Columbia School of Journalism who wish to liberate Tibet. They are the foes of Damodarbhai. Philosophical Thugs, that is what they are, like the patriarchs of the Sangh on the other side of the fence. And that is the name of her website. PhilosophicalThugs.com.

5

Around 11 a.m.

THE ATTACK ON her probably did not last more than a minute. After the initial shock, some firemen had rushed to her rescue and pushed the boys away. An old woman, too, charged at the goons with a handful of debris. A small crowd then had a scuffle with the patriots, who wished to leave anyway. As they left they chanted, 'DaMo. DaMo. DaMo.' Akhila sat in the compound among the injured whom she had come to help. As she opened her bag and took out the bandages and medicines, people watched her in amusement, which was reasonable. It did look as though she had packed the bag to get thrashed.

There were gashes on her face, arms and back; her T-shirt was torn at the shoulder. This was a good place to get beaten up. There were paramedics at hand who attended to her, and they tried to impress her when they learnt she was a student of neurosurgery. She did feel cheap sponging off what was meant for people whose homes had caved in on them.

Someone gave her a shirt, which she wore over the torn T-shirt. A policeman told her that he would take her to the station on his motorcycle to file a complaint, then drop her home, but she did not want to leave the compound. The cop was relieved when she said she did not wish to file a complaint. 'Mad boys,' he said and scooted before she changed her mind. Television journalists asked her for a comment but she refused to talk to them.

The channels must have gone ahead and broadcast the assault anyway, spinning it off as evidence of the newly empowered patriotic thugs. She has been receiving calls and messages from friends. So she has no choice but to call Pa, who is in Bangalore, before he gets to know and his legs begin to vibrate. Poor man, how his women torment him. The first thing she wants to tell him is, 'I am not Ma, I would never become her. So just don't have a heart attack.' But she knows she won't say that.

When she gets him on the phone she tries to sound casual. 'So, some goons attacked me.'

He laughs. 'Academics? Marxists?'

'This was not on Twitter.'

'What do you mean?'

'The other sort of thugs. Don't freak.'

He is speechless. She lets him be.

'Why?' he says, finally. 'Is this about your Damodarbhai thing?' Then a string of questions. 'I am flying back,' he adds.

'Don't don't don't. There were people who drove them away. I am back home now. I'm going to sleep.'

This man has always been easy to lie to in all the three languages they speak at home. Or do fathers only pretend.

She hopes J does not call. At least not for this. The last thing she wants is to endure the compassionate phone call of a former boyfriend who had claimed to have left her because she was reckless. She is tempted to send him a pre-emptive message, but that would be silly. What a mess even lost love is. She switches off her phone.

She has never been assaulted before. She is surprised that what she feels the most is not fear or anger. Instead she feels stupid, naïve and insulted. She even feels her nation let her down, which is funny because the nation has never pretended to be anything better, it has always been honest, always conveyed to her that it was a place held by men and that she was only encroaching. Her bones hurt, the gashes burn, her spine is stiff and her stomach feels as though it is punctured. But she knows she would be alright soon. She begins to perform some basic yogic poses. Three little girls imitate her, more children gather. There is, finally, laughter.

The firemen have given her a place to sit in their nook near the compound wall. They are amused that she does not wish to leave. They have become friendly. They tell her things they cannot tell others, they tell her that they are now only appearing to search for survivors to keep everyone happy. They really do not believe they would find one. At least not with shovels, rods and ropes. But then there is a development.

THE SOLDIERS ARRIVE and swarm the debris. They are wearing huge military-green headphones, and life-detectors as backpacks on which are printed the words 'Air Defence Unit'. The soldiers do not look particularly caring but they are clearly capable, and much fitter than the firemen. They are just a dozen, but they would do. They look as though they have stood on the ruins of lives before, several times. They walk around the debris with metre-long probes, hoping to detect a human sound or any other kind of vibration. It is only them on the debris now – the firemen and residents have withdrawn to the sidelines. A silent crowd watches.

The sun is severe now, so the soldiers convert the nook of the firemen into a shed. Like the firemen, the soldiers, too, grow accustomed to her presence. They probably imagine she is one of the injured, which she is in a way.

As the soldiers continue to walk around the rubble with their life-detectors and probes, their novelty ceases and the crowd begins to murmur again. But then a sudden silence falls. The cause is a soldier, and all he has done is stopped his walk on the debris. The other soldiers are in motion.

The soldier stands on a massive slab of concrete. He is still for several seconds, then he adjusts his headphones. He appears to have got some kind of a signal from below. But moments later he resumes his walk, and the murmurs of the crowd rise again. A minute later another soldier stops and the crowd falls silent, but he, too, resumes his walk. This occurs a few times but increasingly around a portion of the debris. The soldiers are beginning to cluster around the slab of concrete, which is a portion of a top-floor ceiling. Yet another soldier stops and raises his arm, probably to ask the crowd to be quiet or to get the attention of other soldiers. There is silence once again. He becomes alert, and says something. Two soldiers rush to his side. Several residents run up the rubble but the soldiers quickly control the situation and send all civilians back to the sidelines.

As she is in the soldiers' shed she gets first-hand information. There is a live person in the debris. The survivor is too faint to be understood but he or she exists, somewhere deep inside the debris.

The vibrations from the depths of stone must have brought meaning to their relentless walks over the debris, but if the soldiers have become more alert and agile there is no way they can exhibit that, because they must walk slowly, with great patience, running the probes of their life-detectors over the stones.

The news of the survivor spreads through the small crowd in the compound. Some people say that a massive crane is on its way to lift the debris, but the soldiers are not sure if the crane can enter the narrow lane that leads to the site. Even if all the parked cars and trees on the street are cleared, it is unlikely that the crane would be able to make past the compound's narrow entrance. The number of residents on the debris mountain begins to swell and the soldiers are unable to control them. Some of them begin to scream at the soldiers. Akhila takes a while to understand the substance of what they are trying to say. They are asking the soldiers to run their machines over specific portions of the debris that they believe still hold their homes and families. One man yells, 'Sir, I heard my wife and children in the morning. My door number is 209, second floor, it must be there, right there, I can see our cupboard, that's our cupboard.' He looks blank for a few moments, and he says, 'My door number is 209.'

From the crowd a little girl of about six or seven, wearing a blue skirt and a T-shirt that says, in gold, 'Grand', walks up to a soldier and demands that she be allowed to listen to the headphones.

'It might be my mother,' she says. Then she adds diplomatically, 'Or it might be my father.'

'You won't be able to figure out anything, child,' the soldier says but still he puts the headphones on her.

She listens intently. 'Mama, are you there?' Then she says, 'Papa, are you there? This is me. Abha.'

'They can't hear you,' the soldier says. 'This is not a phone.'

Abha ignores him and keeps talking.

In the murmurs of the crowd, Akhila gathers that no one has seen the girl's parents today. The girl was up early for some reason and playing in the compound when the building collapsed. Some neighbours have tried calling the mobile phones of her parents but their phones are not responsive. Both her parents are deep in the rubble.

Abha finally says 'bye' and hands over the headphones to the soldier. The girl ambles around the rubble and begins to collect things – trousers, buckets, a pressure-cooker, various utensils. She picks one object at a time, goes down to the foot of the mound and places it on the ground. She lines up the objects. She is particular about what she takes but there is no clear pattern to what she chooses except that she does not collect any dolls or other such objects that would belong to a child of her age.

She seems happy in her freedom, running, hopping and dancing in the compound. She joins a group of children who are playing a game Akhila does not fully understand. Are their parents, too, buried?

Akhila, finally, decides to walk over the rubble even though she is certain that her every step would squeeze a breath out of someone deep inside. There is a huddle of soldiers on the concrete slab where they had received the signal.

The leader of the squad from the Air Defence Unit is a large jovial man whom everybody calls Major. He has the habit of drawing a soldier to his chest and speaking softly to him as though he was about to say something dirty. He does that to male residents too.

The Major's plan is to drill a narrow tunnel through the debris, about thirty feet long in his rough calculation, to the location of the survivor, who is probably below ground level. A lanky soldier would crawl into the tunnel and pull the person out.

SHE CAN SEE four stray dogs lurking around, sniffing things, preparing for the inevitability of crawling into crevices and seeking the sources of the odours that are yet to reach the humans. The soldiers have been driving away the dogs all day but they keep returning. In the morning they had remembered to be diffident, but they are now changing character. It must be the smell. Do they sense that a master species has fallen? When a soldier tries to drive one away, the mongrel stands his ground and growls, but he eventually relents. This is going to change in a few hours as the bodies embedded in the debris continue to decay. In the night, the dogs will crawl in.

The soldiers have taken hours to make the tunnel. They are not searching for any more survivors. They have accepted that there is only one. All activity is concentrated around the small dark hole on the slope of the debris hill. The mouth of the hole is about two-and-a-half feet across. Three soldiers have been taking turns crawling in and out of the tunnel with heavy equipment.

The soldiers have cordoned off a small area around the hole by arranging pieces of furniture they found in the debris and tying them together – among them sofas and beds made to stand, and several cupboards. Within the ring are the Major and most of his team. When the soldiers had set up the barricades, there was a mob of reporters but their numbers have since thinned. Any other day, such a rescue would be news but not today. Damodarbhai has won. There were fireworks outside, and lots of chanting and screaming.

A soldier who had crawled into the tunnel about thirty minutes ago is yet to emerge. It is the longest a soldier has been in the hole.

When he finally appears he is covered in white dust. He is lean and long and it appears that he was designed to crawl into narrow tunnels. He almost runs to the Major.

'There is a man, sir,' he says. 'About thirty feet into the tunnel, there is a man lodged in the debris. He is conscious but he is in a very bad way. Fortunately he is not inverted. He is in a lying position, sir, his back resting on a fridge, legs straight. His head is slightly raised as though he is on a thick pillow. That's good. A bit of him is buried in debris. Across his legs is a heavy concrete beam. Between the beam and his legs is the leg of another person. A smashed leg. It looks like the leg of a woman, it is wearing an anklet. Must be his wife. The rest of her is buried in the debris. She is surely dead, sir. I think he knows. His eyes are open, sir, he is half-conscious and speaks a few words. I could not get close to him, sir, because there was no space for me to go past the concrete beam on top of his legs. I can see his face but I cannot reach him. But, sir, I know he is mumbling something. I can't hear him but he is saying something.'

'What do you suggest?' the Major asks.

'We should feed him glucose and fruit juice immediately and begin scraping the beam to extricate him. Then we tie a rope around his feet and pull him out.'

'Let's get down to it then.'

'Sir.'

'Yes.'

'We can also chop his legs off, sir.'

The Major considers this.

The soldier says, 'We have to chop off the beam or his legs, sir. If we cut his legs off, we can bring him up.'

'What do you think?'

'It would be easier to chop his legs than the concrete beam, sir. It would be faster.'

'So what are you saying?'

'I don't know, sir,' the soldier says. 'But we have to decide right now or it will be too late. The problem is, the way he is positioned, I would have to put my hand through the space between the beam and the roof and run the saw. There is no space to do it well. And it's too risky, sir. None of us have the training in that sort of a thing. And we will not be able to give him anaesthesia. He has been in there for nearly six hours without food or water. So if we are chopping his legs off we do it clumsily and without giving him anaesthesia.'

'How old is he?'

'I couldn't figure that out. He is covered in dust. He could be forty, fifty. I don't know, sir. But the anaesthesia may kill him. And we don't know yet if he is diabetic and all that.'

'What do you suggest?'

'Sir.'

'What is it?'

'There is a problem, sir. Whatever we decide to do, we need to first feed him glucose. I will not be able to reach his mouth. I can only throw the packets on him, but I don't know if he can move his hands or if he can even follow instructions. I think he has to be fed, sir, I don't think he has much time.'

'You're saying a soldier would not be able to crawl over the beam and reach his mouth.'

'There is not much space between the beam and the roof of the tunnel, sir. But a little boy would be able to crawl in.'

'We can't send a minor in, the whole world will fuck us in our ass.'

'We can send a little man in, sir, a civilian midget or something? A civilian midget who is very fit. Or...' The soldier's face brightens as though it has only occurred to him. 'Or a woman, sir. A strong, small woman might be able to crawl over to him, sir, but if she is not very flexible she can get stuck inside.'

The Major makes some calls. Forget a small fit woman; there are no women in the first place in the reserve force of the Indian army in the entire state of Maharashtra. There are no women in the city's fire department. They now try to trace a female cop, small, strong and flexible, who would not ask them to fuck off.

Akhila takes another look at the dark hole. It is terrifying. There is a good chance that the rescuer, too, would be buried in. It would take just another mild tremor. But there is a man deep inside, he is dying slowly, fully aware of that perhaps and of the fact that his wife's lifeless limb is over him, and he has no space even to thrash about in fear and desperation. He is probably the father of one of the little children milling about. She can give him a long shot at survival. All she needs is courage. Or she can just walk away, which would be a reasonable decision, even a smart decision.

She goes to the Major and says, 'I can try.'

The Major takes a good look at her. She had thought she would have to be persuasive but the man does not dismiss any idea thrown at him.

'She might be able to crawl over the beam, sir,' the soldier says. 'She is small.'

'Are you sure?' the Major asks her.

'I'm an athlete, a trained rock climber, a doctor.'

'You're a doctor?'

'I've never practised but I am as good as a doctor.'

'Going into a tunnel is a bit risky, you know that.'

'Yes. But it's just twenty feet. I can do it.'

'Thirty feet,' the soldier says. 'It's not a steep tunnel, most of it is flat but it gets narrow in places.'

'I'll be able to do it,' she says.

'Crawling into a tunnel is not as easy as it seems,' the Major says, but he is hoping she would still do it.

'I've done it before. I've crawled.'

'In a tunnel like this?'

'No, but I know I can crawl into a tunnel. My muscles know.'

'Things can collapse, things can fall on your head. There is probably a gas leak.'

'I'll do this, Major.'

'How many push-ups can you do?' the Major asks. She laughs. He is serious.

'Twenty in one go,' she says, which is a fact.

'Man push-ups or woman push-ups?'

'Man push-ups.'

The soldiers laugh, but that is because they believe her.

The lean soldier draws a diagram for her. The tunnel is a gentle gradient of varying width, but towards the end it gets a bit steep and at the very end it gets so narrow that she will be able to pass only sideways. Then there is the pod where the man is stuck under the beam. Once she clears the beam, there will be just enough space for her to crawl over him and feed him.

The good news is that the soldiers are carrying impressive Israeli medical kits. She has been rummaging through their stuff. They even have bone marrow syringes. This means she does not have to find the man's veins to give him intravenous injections. She will be able to infuse saline into him by stabbing the needle into his bone.

The word spreads that the young woman who was beaten up a few hours ago by the patriots is setting out to crawl into a tunnel to feed a dying resident in a final stand of the rescuers.

The families of the missing hope it is their man who has been found. They begin to gather around the ring of furniture that guards the mouth of the tunnel. They are not allowed inside the ring.

The soldiers fit Akhila with a helmet, a headlamp, a walkie-talkie and they attach a small bag to her stomach that contains fluids and medication. There is a discussion among the soldiers about tying a rope around her waist, but they eventually decide against it. The rope would tether her to the outside world and help the soldiers pull her out if she faints or is incapacitated in other ways, but it would also increase her circumference and she may not be able to squeeze through the final crevice. She is warned several times that she cannot be in the tunnel for more than a few minutes because the oxygen levels are very low. As she kneels outside the hole, the Major says, 'Forgot to ask you. Do you know how to crawl backwards?'

'What?'

'If you feel giddy, you have to crawl in reverse immediately and head back. You can't turn around, you know that, there is no space to turn around. You have to crawl backwards.'

It had not occurred to her. 'And,' the Major says, 'if you feel giddy, don't wait for it to pass. It may not pass.'

She crawls into the hole, scraping her arms on the rough debris.

6

A Patriarch's Review

PROFESSOR VAID, IN a light half-sleeve shirt and loose trousers, and smelling of herbs, is ready to leave. But he is very early, like old men. It will be a while before the vehicle arrives to take him to the airport.

The chatter of television experts fills his small ascetic home that does not have sounds of its own. The Sangh has won, the Hindu rule is coming. What more can they say? Impoverished women, Muslims and the low castes have voted against Damodarbhai because he terrifies them. They are wise. The patriarchs will have to work harder to confuse them.

He sits in the coir armchair directly under the ceiling fan and hopes that the apparition of the unhappy cook, with his enormous paunch and slow wounded walk, does not pass through the living room. Vaid imagines a more aesthetic presence in his home. It is a woman but not an old woman. Someone more tiring. A young formidable daughter? She has an athletic frame and an incapacity for endearing meekness, and despite being his daughter her world is framed in English. They are foes, they have to be foes. What must they fight over?

About her decadence, perhaps? But are young women as decadent as they claim these days, are they as sexual as men? Can they ever be? The woman who is a lot like a man has to be the thought-experiment of men, like communism, free trade, the Big Bang, black holes and equality, which the world has taken too seriously.

But why does he wish to believe in the impossibility of sex-crazed women? He does not have a daughter.

If he had been in the care of women, he might not have ended up in such a house. With its narrow doorways and foolish arches, it is hideous; its exteriors are worse. The Sangh had conceived it as a guesthouse. The patriots who were given the task decided that it had to be modern but Indian, which is an expectation on a par with the virgin prostitute. The result was a two-storeyed irregular thing whose ground floor has large rectangular glass windows, and the floor above has contiguous saffron arches like the gums of a toothpaste model. There are slim pillars here and there. As it is not colonial nor Hindu nor Islamic nor beautiful in other ways, it is familiar to most patriots as a place that is contemporary. Much thought goes into the ugliness of the great republic. But he can endure it.

Perhaps he should search for something to read instead of dreaming of formidable daughters. He only re-reads these days, but not literature any more, which is a flea market of frailties. People love literature without realizing that such a love is a surrender to the tastes of alpha cultures, patriarchs and leftists. But millions choose to surrender, unflagging in their search for a mention of themselves in the works of others; something, anything that reminds them that the world, despite everything, is about them. Most of reading is probably a mere selfie. But he accepts that people look for their modest biographies in far uglier places than literature – in astrology, blood reports, lipid profiles.

He wonders what Miss Iyer thinks of literature. She has not posted a prank on a novelist yet, but there is one that comes close.

In the film *The Most Expensive House in the World,* Miss Iyer stands on the Kemp's Corner Flyover in Mumbai. She is in tights and an oversized shirt, its sleeves folded, and she is wearing a wig of wiry grey-and-black hair resembling the coiffure of Arundhati Roy.

It is early morning, the traffic is thin, the air is clear and there is sea breeze on the young glowing face of Miss Iyer. In the background looms Antilia, the gigantic home of India's richest man, Mukesh Ambani. It is probably the most expensive home a human has ever built, Miss Iyer tells us. 'And I am about to read a portion from an essay by Arundhati Roy, a writer of Indian origin who actually lives in India, how strange is that.'

The camera shifts to a view of Antilia. The voice of Miss Iyer says, 'This is what Arundhati Roy wrote about the skyscraper home you see in the frame.' She begins to read a piece of prose by Roy, her voice and intonation remarkably close to Roy's English delivery. She tells us how Roy stared back at Antilia, and how funny Roy found the idea of a home that was twenty-seven floors high, with its own gardens and helipads, and its own weather, and six hundred servants. Roy wonders why Ambani was proud and not embarrassed or terrified to own a home like this in a poor nation.

The film cuts to Delhi, to a lush lane in the prime real estate of Jor Bagh. The viewer is transported to the forbidding gates of an enormous modern mansion, which contains the luxurious flat of Arundhati Roy. Miss Iyer is standing on the road with a malnourished woman in a sari and her feral half-naked little daughter whose hair is the colour of cow dung. The security guard, who is seated in a chair outside the gates, looks on with immense interest. Miss Iyer asks the woman, in atrocious Hindi, for her views on the elegant mansion.

'It's so big, so big, such a big house,' the woman says. 'What more can I say? And such big windows. So much wood, so much stone. I think the weather inside must be very cool. That's what people tell me – that the weather inside such homes is very cool. And look at the pretty trees, the plants. So many plants. What more can I say? What can I say about the homes of big people?'

What Mukesh Ambani's home is to Arundhati Roy, Roy's home is to a malnourished woman. So? The accusation of hypocrisy in an Indian socialist and Marxist is not exactly a high intellectual grouse. Miss Iyer is surely not taking all this trouble to laugh at a minor human flaw that should ideally be declared a fundamental human right.

He has been trying to understand Miss Iyer's complexity. The victims of her pranks are not merely liberals, but heroes of the left, heroes who are light as feather. In the battle between presumed good and presumed evil, good is hiring poorly. Does Miss Iyer see the plain fact? Evil is an equal-opportunity society where the darkest rise. Liberal heroes, on the other hand, are made in a very different sort of place, a place where the gentry suffocate honest competition. Here the midgets rise. What chance do they have against naturally selected arch-villains?

The Sangh is grey. It is not constricted by unnatural moralities, hence has exceptional freedoms to get things done.

7

Around 1:30 p.m.

THIS IS A RARE reversal of social roles in the republic. Normally, in circumstances like this, people like her would employ people like the man in the debris to do all the crawling.

A few feet into the tunnel her shoulders begin to ache, but it is not an unfamiliar pain. She was worried that the attack on her may have left her with injuries that she may have underestimated, but she seems a lot like her usual self. She is strong, she knows that, and she has a genius core.

There is a powerful stink in the tunnel, a damp revolting smell. The air is particulate. There are electric wires hanging from the roof and she hopes the first thing the firemen did was cut off the power supply. Her chest moves over something stiff, something hard and rubbery in a very human way. She feels as though she is being groped. She looks down to train the headlamp on the object.

It is the hand of a buried human.

In her panic she bangs her helmet against the roof and thrashes her body about trying to turn around, which she realizes she cannot. She begins to feel giddy. She stops moving, and calms her breath. It has been only seconds since she entered the tunnel and if she passes out now it would be a while before the soldiers realize something has gone wrong.

She begins a slow backward crawl. When she emerges from the tunnel the soldiers help her out and make her lie on her back. They don't say anything, which is a relief. They probably did not expect this to work in the first place. She glares at the soldier who had drawn her the map of the tunnel. 'There is a human hand jutting out, you know,' she says.

'Yes, yes,' he says with a chuckle. 'I forgot to tell you.'

'Tell me everything.'

'That's the only thing I forgot.'

The soldiers laugh.

They are surprised when she prepares to crawl again. This time she is a bit faster. She shuts her eyes to endure the moment when her body will slither over the hand. The moment passes, she crawls on. She hopes the roof will not cave in. Everything above her is an accidental arrangement of loose slabs of concrete. Her walkie-talkie crackles.

'Okay?' the Major asks.

'Okay,' she says.

'As you get deeper, we may not be able to communicate,' he says.

When she spots the far end of the tunnel she realizes that it is narrower than she had imagined. A few feet from the crevice she sees the man in the light of her headlamp. He is exactly as the soldier had mentioned. Lying with his legs straight, a concrete beam over his knees. Squashed between him and the beam is the naked leg of a woman. The rest of the woman, if it exists, is buried. The man's head is covered in dust and blood. He has a moustache. His head is raised, which is lucky for him. His aimless eyes stare at a spot that has no special meaning. He looks calm and lost. There is not much room above him. This has to be the worst that can happen to a person.

The lean soldier was almost certain that she would be able to squeeze herself between the beam and the roof. When she looks at the gap, she wonders if she is really that small. But if she manages to get past the gap, there is enough room inside for her to take care of him.

When she reaches his naked feet, she shouts, 'Can you hear me?' She says it first in Marathi, then in Hindi. No real Indian would use English to break ice with a man buried in debris; it is as though such calamities can happen only to the vernacular. His lips move but she cannot hear him.

His feet are cold and the pulse is slow, but not as slow as she had feared. She has a clear view of only inches of his lower limbs. The rest is under the beam. She tries not to look at the leg of the woman, but then she stares at it to get used to the corpse. She wonders if the woman was his wife or his child.

She feels a portion of the man's tibia, sprays antiseptic and stabs the bone marrow needle into the bone. And she twists the syringe's grip until she feels the needle has reached the marrow. There is no reaction from him. He continues to mumble as she slowly injects the saline. She repeats the procedure on the other leg.

She takes out a packet of glucose water from her pouch and throws it over the beam, to his side. She discards the pouch, and crawls over the beam one leg first. She clears the gap just about, slithers on to the other side of the beam, and crawls over the man. There is space just for two tightly squeezed bodies. She has never crawled over a man without a sexual mission.

His body does not appear to register the weight, but his lips stop moving. She does not know the extent of his internal injuries, she might be killing him by bearing down on him. Her face is now just an inch over his. His eyes are wide open but they are not focused on her. It is as though they are observing something deep within himself. Despite the layers of dust and dried blood, she can tell he is not very old. He is probably in his late thirties or early forties, and in good shape.

'Can you hear me,' she says in Hindi. 'What's your name?'

Maybe he is from the south? She speaks to him in Tamil, and in such bad Malayalam that it would be a torture to a dying Malayalee.

'Blink if you hear me,' she says.

He does not respond. His breath is shallow. She cannot be on top of him for too long. She is also blocking his air supply. She squeezes the glucose from the Tetra Pak into his mouth. He drinks, which is a relief. His body figures that sugar has arrived and it shudders in desperation. He gulps it down, and begins to mumble. He is certainly saying something. His voice has no strength, he speaks from his lips, there is no movement in his throat. He is probably saying, 'Get off my chest, bitch.' She puts her ear to his mouth.

'What time is it? What time is it? What time is it?' That's what he says. He mumbles in lousy Mumbaiya Hindi with a heavy slur, but he says 'time' in English.

It is odd that he must ask her a question. Of all the things he can say, a question, and that too 'what time is it?' There is no doubt in her mind that he is delirious and non-responsive to instructions. He is in no position to follow commands, let alone ask a question because a question seeks an answer and his mind cannot be at that level of communication. Yet he asks, again, 'What time is it?'

'One in the afternoon,' she says.

As she had expected he repeats the question. She yells the answer. That makes him go silent. But then he repeats the question one more time. Then his lips deliver a different set of words. She puts her ear to his mouth. At first she feels he is not making any sense but slowly his words gather force and meaning.

8

A Telephone Conversation

PROFESSOR VAID'S PHONE has been ringing all day. He has ignored all the calls but the man whose name now flashes on the screen is too important. And, he always has good reasons to call.

'Professor.'

'AK.'

'Can we talk?'

'Where are you?'

'Delhi. I can't be anywhere else today. Have you been watching the news?'

'Should we call it news? It's the most predictable day of our lives.'

'Women still hate us, Professor.'

'You must be referring to the election results.'

AK has a nasal laugh. And he laughs often. By his laughter alone one would not guess he is a national treasure.

'Do you have the time to talk, Professor?'

'Go on.'

'This morning a building collapsed in Mumbai.'

'Strange you should say that.'

'Why is it strange?'

'A boy in the shakha said the same thing a few hours ago. A building has fallen in Mumbai. It seems to be the most insignificant news today but looks like everyone is going to tell me about it.'

'Why did the boy tell you about the building?'

'It's nothing important.'

'Tell me.'

'It really is not worth your time, AK. A building fell, so?'

'There were mild tremors in Mumbai. It's possible that several old buildings have fallen. Actually that can't be true. That would be big news.'

'It doesn't matter how many buildings fell.'

'It doesn't matter. What's interesting, Professor, is that the guys in the Intelligence Bureau are very excited.'

'What happened?'

'There is a man trapped in the debris of the fallen building. He is probably dying. But he has been mumbling. He drifts in and out of consciousness, but when he is awake he mumbles.'

'What does he mumble?'

'That's the thing. At first, he was saying, "What's the time?", "What's the time?" The same thing over and over again. Then he said that a man is about to leave his home. He would be carrying explosives on him. He is going to blow up things today.'

'Oh.'

'Yes.'

'Where is that man going?'

'I don't know much right now, Professor. I just got off the phone. I have an informant who is with the Crime Branch but he is not on the site. He is on his way to the location. He is on the phone with some people who are on the site. So, what I have is not first-hand information. I am still trying to grow eyes and ears on the site. The details are very, very sketchy.'

'This man in the debris, AK. He is not saying someone is on his way to plant a bomb. He is saying a man is about to set out. He is saying a man is about to leave his home.'

'Yes.'

'That's very specific.'

'Yes. He is vague about some things, specific about some things. But that's how people are even when they are not buried in debris.'

'How does this guy, this guy who is in the debris, know about the terrorist?'

'You may have guessed, Professor.'

'He is involved?'

'It looks that way. This is how I see it: a terror coordinator or an accomplice was at his home this morning. He was supposed to join another man and blow up stuff. But his building collapsed. Now he is in the debris, in some sort of a final delirium, so he is blurting out real-time information about the movements of a terrorist.'

'I think he is just blabbering. Maybe in his final moments he has remembered a film he saw with a beautiful woman.'

'No, Professor, I think he is giving away the details of a terror plot.'

'You see terror in everything, AK. That's your job.'

'I am just a retired cop.'

'You're the next National Security Advisor.'

'That's confidential information.'

'So you're taking the dying man in the debris seriously?'

'Yes.'

'Very seriously?'

'Yes.'

'The building, is it in a Muslim ghetto?'

'No. It's Prabhadevi. As Hindu as it gets, but you know Mumbai. There are all kinds of people in places that nobody would guess are places.'

'AK, there is a man in the debris and he is saying something. That much I can understand. But who is listening?'

'I don't know, yet. But what I imagine is that the man is stuck under a huge concrete slab and a group of rescuers, maybe firemen and soldiers, are able to hear him rambling.'

'And he's saying that there is going to be some fireworks today. That's a tribute to this day, isn't it?'

'I'm getting a call, Professor. I am going to call you back.'

A few minutes later, AK calls again.

'Professor, can we talk?'

'Go on.'

'My guy is yet to reach the site but he called with some information. We don't know the name of our man in the debris, yet. He is not responding to questions. I think he is slipping away. But he has been mentioning a name. We presume that's the name of the man who is about to blow up something somewhere. Jamal.'

'They're all called Jamal.'

AK lets out his nasal laugh.

'Jamal lives in Mumbra,' he says.

'According to the man in the debris?'

'Yes.'

'How far is Mumbra from Mumbai?'

'It's a distant suburb. Two hours from the building that collapsed.'

'A Muslim hole?'

'Yes.'

'So our Jamal is going someplace.'

'He has not yet left home, according to our man.'

'If our friend is under a concrete slab, as you guess, a whole lot of people, not just the firemen and soldiers, must be hearing him. Isn't the information a bit too sensitive for too many people, too many bystanders.'

'That's my concern, too, but something is totally bizarre about the whole thing.'

'What?'

'Not many people seem to know about this. A lot of very senior cops in Mumbai don't know. The media is definitely clueless. There appears to be some kind of control in place.'

AK says he will call again, and he does. This time he is calmer.

'Professor.'

'I was waiting for your call.'

'I have six men on the site now. Cops, Bureau guys, one Major. They're all feeding me. Their information is now consistent.'

'So what is going on?'

'After the building fell, the firemen poked around a bit, but then the soldiers flew in from Pune in a chopper. They were carrying acoustic life-detectors. And they detected the vibrations of a man deep in the debris. They dug a tunnel and they found their man.'

'So that's why very few people know about this.'

'Yes, but there is a complication. The man is stuck under a heavy beam. He is in such a position that a soldier cannot reach his upper body because the gap between the beam and the roof of the tunnel is very narrow. So, they sent a girl in.'

'A civilian?'

'Yes, a civilian but the athletic type. She is a doctor, too. Perfect.'

'She is a doctor?'

'A student but postgraduate type.'

'Alright.'

'The man is very weak, he is very, very faint. The girl has to put her ear to his mouth.'

'So everything we know, AK, is what the girl has been telling the soldiers?'

'Yes.'

'There is nothing that anyone else has heard. It's all just the girl telling us?'

'Why do you ask?'

'I'm trying to understand. That's all.'

'You asked the same question twice, Professor.'

'It's nothing.'

'What's on your mind, Professor?'

'Nothing important. Go on.'

'That's it for now.'

'He has not said more?'

'Nothing more. One Jamal is about to leave his house. He is going to blow up something somewhere. We don't know the place yet.'

'Jamal who lives in Mumbra. That's all we know?'

'Jamal. Mumbra. Yes.'

'Jamal. Mumbra. Is that enough for the cops to be on to him?'

'Depends on the intel they already have and the men they are stringing upside down right now. They might be on to him already.'

9

Miss Laila, Armed and Dangerous

THERE ARE FACES only an Indian can make. In his short life of twenty-eight years, Mukundan has never breathed the air of any other nation but he knows there are faces only an Indian can make. Like that baffled face when he is shocked by the most rational outcome of his own actions. He crosses the road like a cow, and he is startled by a truck. A vehicle on the road? How? He walks across the railway track, and he finds a train hurtling towards him. A train on a railway track? He is stunned. Cops who do not wear bulletproof vests break into a house to fight militants, and they are shot in their paunches. They stagger out looking bewildered. That baffled face, when boys fall off trains because they were dangling from the doorways, when illegal homes built on infirm soil collapse, when pilgrims are squashed in annual stampedes inside narrow temples.

But then the foes of the republic, too, are delivered the face. Sooner or later they all find it. Enemies of humanity, criminals, psychotics. The republic is a giant prank. It lures all into believing that they can do anything and get away with it.

And they do get away with a lot. But then one day, inevitably, surprise.

Mukundan is waiting on the street for a man. If he is waiting like this, in a small private car hired by the Intelligence Bureau, six licence plates stashed in the boot, it means someone has run out of luck. You can say Mukundan is a bearer of surprise.

He combs his hair, studying the rear-view mirror. He enjoys the act of combing. It is meaningless and relaxing.

He is about a hundred metres away from the building where Jamal lives. Somewhere on the fourth floor, the top floor, Jamal is probably chatting with his wife. There is much love in that house. That is the information. Jamal has three little sons. It would be so simple if men like Jamal were bachelor psychopaths. But they usually are not.

Mukundan is at the wheel of the WagonR, which is parked on the edge of the narrow bustling street. He has lived in Mumbai almost all his life, for twenty-five years, but he has never been to this hellhole before; he has never even uttered the word 'Mumbra' ever. Mumbra, it turns out, is an enchanted place where fragrant streams flow, divine food lines the alleys and wild lovers romp on fruits. But this is from a pig's point of view.

Hindus would say it is a filthy colony. When Hindus say that, it has a clear meaning.

'Why are Muslims so filthy?' Damodarbhai said a few weeks ago, standing on a stage. Fifty thousand people burst out laughing. The crowds cheered him on to say more and he gave them a long analysis of why they are filthy. He said, 'The Hindu man and wife abide by our family planning slogan:

We Two, Ours Two.' The crowds clapped as though they were all joint inventors of contraception, but they were so excited because they knew what was coming. 'A Muslim man takes four wives, and what do they all say in the bedroom, "We two, ours twenty-five." One day, my friends, there will be more Muslims in our country than us.'

Damodarbhai says things in public that most leaders only say in private. That is all he needs to do, it is that easy to be him. People have employed him to say some things aloud. If everybody who is given a mike, especially the righteous, if those intellectuals speak the simple truths of a nation, however unpleasant, Damodarbhai would have had to work harder to rise. He would have risen anyway, but not so easily. The way things are, he has to just speak the mind of his people. Some days, after he speaks the mind of a Hindu, the Hindu's mind may not seem so impressive. But most of the time he reassures his people that they are not alone in their thoughts, that very powerful men who have got somewhere in life have similar views. That is what Damodarbhai is – he is not right, he is not wrong, he is a secret thought that people have already thought.

Mukundan would not deny that there are some similarities between him and Damodarbhai. He, too, is a soldier of the Sangh but he has not worn the uniform since adolescence. To climb up the ranks of the Sangh, as Damodarbhai has shown, you don't have to always flaunt the stupid elephant shorts. You need to just remain a man. That, Mukundan plans to do. And like Damodarbhai, he is a poet. He has not shown anyone his poems but who can deny he is a poet. He is probably not very good, he admits. The major literary flaw in him is that he is incapable of whining, he finds that humiliating even in a poem no one else is going to see. All his poems are tributes to the strong, and to himself. Like Damodarbhai's poems, which are usually about Damodarbhai as a tiger, Damodarbhai as a lion, Damodarbhai as a busy honeybee.

The filthy street teems with stunted young men in tight jeans, old men with orange beards, a few women here and there in hijab, little children in school uniforms walking carefully in the gaps between garbage piles and open puddles. Lots of little girls. Everywhere there are happy little girls in oversized uniforms. The image of girls going to school, or even if they are returning, has something triumphant about it. Whose triumph he does not know, but somebody's triumph. Here they are a swarm, they are walking, on cycles, on the motorbikes of their fathers, in rickshaws, there are a dozen of them stuffed inside one stationary autorickshaw, some of them sitting on an iron-rod barrier, their bottoms jutting out, one such bottom being sniffed by a passing cow, who may be consumed soon, discreetly.

One reason why the Muslim population is growing faster than the Hindu, Damodarbhai would never say it aloud, is that Muslims don't kill their girls in the womb. So many girls have been killed it is now evident in plain sight – not only as streets and villages and railways stations filled only with men, but as eerie stares.

A few months ago, when his niece was born, Mukundan began carrying the infant around the lanes of Parel. One morning, as he walked past a long queue of women who were standing outside a temple, he noticed some of them staring with a sad smile. They were staring at him and the girl in his arms who they probably imagined was his daughter. He was struck by the faces of the women who stared because they reminded him of accidental murderers in custody, and he wondered what crime the women may have committed and why they were looking at the child and him in that manner. Were they forced to kill their own girls, was that why they were gaping at a man walking so happily with a little girl in his arms? He has seen that dark gaze many times on the streets. That stare is in the heart of a poem that he has been struggling to write. It is a poem about him carrying an infant girl and walking across the great nation, across towns and villages, up the hills and on the banks of holy rivers, holding aloft the giggling girl and stirring the peace of fragrant guilty households. But he is not a good poet, the honest words just won't come.

FINALLY, JAMAL APPEARS. He walks out of the building carrying a black travel bag.

Mukundan is always fascinated by this moment, the moment when an image becomes a person.

People look reasonable in photographs, but they are usually misshapen in the flesh. They don't mean to disappoint, obviously, or to trick. It is just the way things are. In his photographs, Jamal looks fine as most people do. In person, he is not a man who is aligned well. His left shoulder is higher than his right, his neck is thick and short and he has the unquiet walk of a man who is lurking more than passing through. But he does look a lot like the man he wants the world to believe he is. A decent, educated Malayalee, an electrical subcontractor whose small firm lays cables in a dozen offices, a small businessman who dabbles in many things and feeds his happy family with his minor enterprises. This is not a front. He is all this, like millions of men. Most terrorists, like poets, have regular jobs, insipid jobs.

Jamal walks to a blue Indica that is among the many vehicles parked on the street. It is a second-hand car he had bought a few weeks ago with cash. That is the information with the Bureau. He flings the travel bag on the back seat. The way he does that, it is as though there are just clothes in it. Where is the bomb? It's unlikely that he is strapped to it. Maybe it is in the boot of the car?

After Jamal gets into the driver's seat he ducks to have a clear look at something through the passenger window. He is looking for something or someone in his building. It must be the balcony of his home – he wants to have a glimpse of home. A father of three little boys who thinks he is coming back.

The information with the Bureau is that Jamal will hit the National Highway and head towards Ahmedabad, five hundred kilometres down that road. All Mukundan has to do is tail him till the Vasad Tollbooth, about ninety kilometres short of Ahmedabad. Jamal will not be crossing the tollbooth a free man. He will not be arrested either. He will be abducted by the Intelligence Bureau and taken to a safe house. Every ounce of information will be squeezed from his body.

Mukundan will not be a part of the abduction. He is not so important. His assignment is, as always, to shadow until more important men take over.

His life has been filled with simple expectations from the world, and long waits. He is good at waiting.

In the act of waiting you watch events unfold. Events are usually the creation of people in haste. In waiting you watch them win, until an opportunity arises to intervene decisively. Then, surprise. He can wait for as long as he needs to. He hopes waiting is an art as some writers claim. That would make him an artiste. But he really does not believe that. He does not believe many beautiful things writers say.

He begins to drive. It is a slow congested road and there are half a dozen vehicles between Jamal and him.

Most days, Mukundan would say that people are not as unique as they imagine, that there are only a few types of people and the whole world is a repetition of the types. But he has never known a man like Jamal. That can mean the intel about him is not complete. But what is known about him casts him as an unusual suspect.

Jamal is not his name. Until eight years ago, he was Praveen Namboodiri. He was a Hindu, a high-caste from north Kerala, like Mukundan, who was raised by good, responsible parents. His father lives on a farm a thousand miles away. Jamal's mother died two years ago of cancer. How does a high-caste Hindu become a Muslim? As things stand, Muslims are lower than the untouchables. It is harder for them to find jobs and homes unless they choose to stick with other Muslims. And they are always suspects even if people are not sure what the crime is. At least the untouchables are recognized as 'the oppressed', whatever that means. The Hindus were bad to them, everyone knows, everyone accepts, and society has been forced to make up to them. But there is no such concession for Muslims. So why would a Brahmin choose to become a Muslim in a country where the roll of the dice is everything?

The Brahmin had fallen in love with a Muslim girl. To win her hand he chose to convert. What an idiot. Still, the girl's parents did not yield. But the girl accepted. A man loves a woman, he pursues her, he pursues her parents as he must, and he sacrifices his religion and his caste to win her. This Mukundan can accept because no matter what some scholars may say, there is such a thing as love. You can defame love by calling it madness, which only confirms its existence. But how can a man who converted to Islam out of love for a woman become an Islamic terrorist? It does not make sense.

There is a lame Bureau theory that says Jamal was infuriated by the riot that almost everybody believes Damodarbhai had planned. But that does not explain the transformation of Jamal into a terrorist. Perhaps he is in it just for the money. Maybe he is not really going to blow up anything. He probably is not even carrying a bomb. Mukundan has tried to find the source of the intel on Jamal but nobody has been able to give a clear answer. And, what were the set of events that made the Bureau rush Mukundan to Mumbra to shadow this man? Nobody appears to know.

Maybe Jamal is only running supplies of a terror cell. Maybe he was lured into this by a good talker. But even this does not make complete sense. Why would a man risk everything he holds dear and go down this path? And Jamal has much to hold dear.

Jamal's car is fifty metres ahead, and Mukundan can see the man's contours. A young father, a young husband who pursued his childhood sweetheart. That is what he is, apart from other things.

Mukundan has never chased a woman. Even in that department he waits. He is not a romantic perhaps. That way he is not harmful to women. He wonders what it is to pursue love. Men who chase women, what is it that they whisper to their sweethearts? Do they ever speak the truth, which includes speaking all the truths? Do they say, 'I will always be yours'? That makes him laugh, probably because he is alone in a car and people do things when they are alone in a car just because they can. 'Sweetheart, I'll always be yours because no one else might want me or I might be too frightened to stray, for that is what faithful men are, darling, unwanted or cowards.' How can the Romeos be so sure that the women they seduce would not be happier with other men, better men? Jamal's wife, for instance, would be destroyed in a few hours. Because of him. The romantics are probably men who have the gift of pomposity, selfish little men with an evolutionary advantage in a world where there is another kind of men, men who wait.

As Mukundan is available and the world of lovers and spouses such a miserable place, he hopes to become a beacon for at least women in doomed relationships, women who have seen through the farce of the men who pursued them. Once he discovers a way to let women find him, his life will be crowded with women, hopefully happy women – there have to be happy women – happy women who will regard him as an object of sex. But then that is not how women are made, no matter what the posh may say on television chat shows.

He is a fan of a woman who writes a weekly column in *Malayala Manorama* on the strange theme, 'English books that will never translated into Malayalam'. Last week she reviewed a scholarly book, *Why Women Have Sex,* written by two serious professors. After a decade of research they believe that women mate for exactly 237 reasons. One of the reasons why women have sex, apparently, is that they want to. And love has nothing to do with it. The columnist mentions this with some sort of triumph. But there are 236 other reasons why women have sex. Treacherous reasons, terrifying reasons. Reasons that even women do not know are reasons.

He has to be vigilant. A life without meaning is fragile, it can collapse any moment into purpose.

Something is wrong. Jamal has skipped the turn. He is not headed towards the highway. He is going deeper into Mumbra. What's going on? Has he got a whiff of the tailing?

The space between the blue Indica and Mukundan's WagonR has accumulated four cars, a dozen motorbikes, a lost ass, and a water tanker chased by a gang of urchins who are trying to open the tap in the rear, ignoring the threats of the driver that he will kill them.

After about five minutes the Indica stops by the wayside, in front of a small bakery. Mukundan contemplates stopping. That would not be conspicuous in the chaos. If he continues, he would be ahead of Jamal in less than a minute. He decides to keep moving. It is never a bad idea to shadow a man by being ahead of him.

As he overtakes the parked Indica, he gets the clearest view yet of Jamal, who is calm but whose gaze is fixed on something ahead. Moments later, Mukundan sees what Jamal sees. A striking young woman in a light-brown salwar-kurta crosses the road. She is crying in a tense, angry sort of way. She is marching across the street with a small plastic bag that is stuffed with things. She does not have a handbag, which is odd. Almost every woman can afford a handbag these days. She is too preoccupied with her immediate trauma to look where she is going and she bangs into a cyclist. The cyclist, an old man, shouts at her but she keeps walking. After crossing the road she turns left, towards Mukundan's car. She seems to know where she is going. She walks past his car, towards the Indica, which is about twenty metres behind him. In the rear-view he sees the front passenger door of the Indica open. The young woman gets in and shuts the door, but the Indica does not move. They are talking. It has to be about the reason why she is crying, what else can they be talking about? After about a minute, Mukundan is still not too far ahead of Jamal on the slow road. He is certain that the girl will leave the idling car soon. But then the Indica moves and merges with the traffic.

Mukundan does not have to try too hard to let Jamal overtake him. As the Indica passes him, he gets another glimpse of the young woman. She is not crying any more. She is a pretty girl with a very red nose. Would she like his poems?

She must get away from that car. She has to just open the door and walk away. That is all she needs to do. He hopes she has nothing to do with terror. He wonders why he hopes that.

About ten minutes later, the Indica enters a narrow lane and stops outside Patel School for Girls, which is a pink building of four floors that stands behind a high iron gate. The young woman gets out of the car without the bag, jogs to the gates and appears to argue with the security guard, who eventually lets her in. Mukundan hopes this is her escape, but Jamal does not leave. The Indica waits. She returns a few minutes later, looking a bit happier. She smiles as she runs towards the car.

In a few minutes, Jamal and the girl are on the highway, racing towards Ahmedabad, into a trap where some deadly cops wait for a blue Indica with the registration number MH02-DJ-687.

What must have lured her into the car? What hope, what lies?

He waits for an hour to see if the girl will get dropped off somewhere on the highway. That does not happen. He has no choice but to make the call.

'Sir.'

'Yes.'

'Jamal is on the highway.'

'Good.'

'He is in the blue Indica.'

'Good.'

'Sir.'

'What's the matter?'

'Sir, there is a girl with him. There is a girl in the car.'

Boss is so taken aback he lets out a sound that is certainly not a word.

'What do you mean there is a girl with him?'

'He picked up a young woman, sir, and she is in the car with him. It appears that she is an acquaintance, very close maybe. She is family or lover or an employee or something like that.'

Boss is silent, which is not unusual. But the man is silent for too long. Then he begins to bark at someone. Boss's reaction suggests that he has no clue about the girl, she was not on the radar.

She probably has no idea what she has got into. She is Jamal's armour, that is what she is. Jamal imagines that the system would not take a man who is with a young woman in a little blue hatchback seriously.

What does he think, the State fights terror by standing on the roadside and looking for solitary men in SUVs?

'Sir?'

'I am here.'

'Sir, what do we do about the girl?'

'This is going to be messy.'

10

Laila

DEFINE 'A TON of bricks'. All Aisha Raza has to do is swallow her pride, concede the point to the English textbook and write the only permissible answer on the answer sheet: 'a great weight'. She does not deny that 'a ton of bricks' is 'a great weight', but a ton of bricks would weigh the same as a ton of peacock feathers. So 'a ton of bricks' cannot be about weight alone. But the world is surely smarter than she is. A 'ton' probably has other meanings, meanings that she does not know yet. But still.

Aisha is a bit cranky this morning. It is not about the English test at all. It is not about what would follow either, even though that would be unpleasant. What is bothering her is the incident at home in the morning. Laila was going somewhere with Jamal and Mother went all Taliban. He seems to be a gentle person but it is also true that he has been to jail more than once for thrashing people. As much as Aisha is convinced that her mother is wrong about almost everything, she herself is tormented by the thoughts of Laila in the company of a grown-up man, let alone a man who has seen jail.

'Time,' the teacher shouts as though he is going to recite an angry poem about time. All the girls line up to hand in the answer sheets. Aisha prepares to survive the next few minutes.

Every day, towards the end of the English class, a student has to read out 'an original essay in good English' on the theme, 'My Family'. It is her turn today. She can lie about her family but then everybody knows the facts. If everybody knows the facts, what is there to worry. Still, it is going to be humiliating when she herself spells out the details. She is overreacting perhaps. It is going to be bad only for the first few seconds.

No miracle occurs and Aisha finds herself standing in front of the overcrowded, sweating class of forty-two girls. 'My family,' she says. There are giggles already but that is just Mala, who is a cow. 'My family consists of my mother and six sisters.'

The class erupts in giggles. It's a lot of sisters, Aisha does not dispute that. Worse, she has made a tactical mistake. The pause is too long. 'And one brother.' There is disastrous laughter. Her essay sounds a bit funny even to her.

'Anyone else? Anyone you forgot?' the teacher asks. And there is more laughter than is necessary.

These days everybody is worried that Muslims are 'reproducing like rabbits'. Yesterday, the maths teacher wrote this sum on the board: 'Assume the fact that Hindus form 80 per cent of the Indian population and Muslims form 15 per cent. If the number of Hindus grows by 50 per cent every decade and the number of Muslims doubles every decade, after how many decades would there be more Muslims than Hindus in India?' The man has been asking all of Patel School for Girls the same sum, even little kids.

Anyone else in her family? Anyone she forgot?

'I had a father,' she says. 'Two years ago he died in a road accident when he was on his way to get us sweets. I love my father.' There is silence as she expected. It is for this reason she had invoked him even though it makes her sad to talk about him.

'I love all my sisters but I'm closest to Laila. She is very, very clever, and physically stronger than she looks. She is not the eldest sister. Our eldest sister is married and does not live with us.' On an impulse she decides to play to the gallery. 'She has no children.' But nobody seems to have got the significance of that bit of information. 'Laila is the second oldest. She is nineteen. After her is my only brother. I come next. I've three younger sisters. I'm their boss. And my boss is Laila.'

Aisha is still distracted by the gloom of remembering her father, who was a good man, a jovial man. She almost never talks about him except when Laila gets into the mood and forces everyone in the house to talk about Father. The children then sit in a circle on the floor and recount memories and conversations. 'Don't be afraid to repeat stuff,' Laila would say. It's surprising that often they come up with things they had not remembered earlier. Laila says that people should not go quiet about their dead, they must instead keep talking about them. But it is hard.

She wonders how Laila would react if she knew that Aisha had used Father to get some sympathy from the class. Laila might not be so cross. In fact, she might think it was smart. Laila herself is a bit of a rogue.

Aisha had exploited Father not only to get some dignity back but also to reassure people that Muslims do die. Maybe she should also have added, 'Muslims die in many ways. Muslims die in "spontaneous riots", too, so don't worry too much about our population.'

The smiling face of Damodarbhai flashes in her mind. She has to stop her essay to recover. In those riots, three cousins died – two boys in their late teens and a girl who was sixteen. When the riots began in Ahmedabad, many Muslims ran to the house of a big Muslim politician, a very old man. The mobs gathered around the old man's house. Their numbers grew through the morning but the cops never arrived. The mobs then began to pelt stones. The old man called many people in the government, begging for help. But there were just cops with sticks outside his house and they could not do anything to control the mob.

The old politician called Damodarbhai, too. Damodarbhai was chief minister after all, but Damodarbhai asked him to get lost. Then the old man took his own gun and shot at the mob. Big mistake. The mob barged in and hacked every Muslim they could find. They hacked and burned. They hacked the old man into so many pieces no part of him was ever found.

What if Laila had been in the old man's house that day? Aisha is going to cry, she knows that. She finds it odd that she must always think of only Laila in distress. There are others she loves, including herself, but it is always Laila.

The day Damodarbhai became chief minister yet another time and everybody started saying that he was destined to become prime minister and run the whole country and not merely a state, all the children in her home were terrified. Jaan, who was four then, went to sleep with two slices of cucumber on her eyes. Even now she does that when she is very scared or tense. Aisha crawled under her parents' bed and refused to come out. Mother got tired of trying to lure her out and finally shoved a broom under the bed. 'Since you are there, why don't you clean the cobwebs, too.' But Laila stayed with her all day. Not under the bed but a few feet away, lying on the floor, resting her head on her palm, like Vishnu. It was a Sunday, the day she is not very busy. They talked for two hours about movies, food and Mumbai. Aisha ate under the bed, lying on her belly.

Laila studies science in Guru Nanak Khalsa college in Mumbai. She travels up and down three hours every weekday to attend college. Laila says poor people, like them, should learn to love science because science is more equal and fair than arts. Aisha understands. The thing about science is that if you are smart no one can say you are not smart. But Laila does not plan to become a scientist. She does not have the time to keep dissecting frogs for years, she wants to start earning a lot of money fast. 'A lot of money.' She plans to take the MBA exams next year.

Laila runs the house. She takes tuitions for schoolchildren at home. She also designs and stitches salwar-kameez that she manages to sell to some stores. Most of the clothes that the family wears have been made by Laila. The cream kurta she was wearing this morning was made by her last week. The only thing Laila likes about Pakistan is the way they cut salwars. 'But they don't know how to cut churidars.' Laila also works in Jamal's company but Aisha does not fully understand what she does there. Something to do with accounting.

Once a month, Laila takes her to south Mumbai or Bandra and they watch flashy girls. It is fun. Laila says that flashy girls always remind her of men. 'They are so lucky, so lucky.' Sometimes Laila looks carefully at fancy young people sitting in glass restaurants or going in cars. Her face then grows a bit sad. Maybe she too wants to have fun like others her age instead of doing so many odd jobs to run a family. It really is unfair that Laila has to carry so much burden at nineteen. Her family is a 'ton of bricks'.

It must be because Laila is so precious to all of them, every moment of Aisha's life she fears that something bad will happen to her. Aisha is very imaginative when she thinks of all the things that can happen. Laila may fall off the train, get run over by a truck; a skinny nervous Romeo may throw acid on her face, thugs might abduct her. Or Jamal might shoot her in the head after an argument. Or a riot can break out and that has its own possibilities. She wishes Laila were a bit religious at least. They need God in that house. But Laila thinks no woman is religious. 'They are all just pretending. Imagine an old man peering into your life all the time. Which woman would want that?'

Her fear that Laila would be destroyed in horrible ways is worse than usual today. Early morning she woke up to a nasty fight between Mother and Laila. The other children slept through it, but not for long. Aisha sat in a corner of the room and brushed her teeth slowly, watching the show. The issue, she figured, was serious. Laila was going to Malegaon to meet some perfume merchants or something like that, and she was going to spend a whole night in a hotel. That was bad enough but Laila was going with Jamal in the second-hand car that he bought last month. Just Jamal and Laila – to Malegaon. Serious matter.

'It's not like we're sharing a room,' Laila said.

'Which nineteen-year-old girl would go out of town with a man?' Mother said.

'I've been to Malegaon before.'

'But not with a man alone. Or that's what I hope. And how dare you tell me this now, a moment before you are to leave. You could have told me yesterday. You're obviously not asking my permission. You're informing me, that's all.'

'Jamal decided to take me along just now. I'm going on work. Work. Work.'

'Just because you run this house, just because you bring in the money, you have no respect for me.'

'Don't say such things.'

'That man is not a straightforward person. I can see it in his eyes. Something wrong about him.'

'He is a good man.'

'If your father was alive, would you dare to go up to him and say you're going out of town with a man?'

'Yes.'

'I hope you're not a prostitute.'

Then both started crying. It is rare for Laila to cry, rarer still for her to scream. 'It's tough, life is so tough,' she yelled. 'I'm trying to do something. I can't be like those girls who just lie around because everything will fall nicely in place. I have to work.'

It is not unusual for people to scream in Rashid Complex.

It happens all the time, but very rarely in that house, because it does not have a man, or sisters-in-law.

'Laila,' Mother screamed, 'you get careless with men, you end up dead in this country. That's how it is.'

That made Aisha go mad. 'Don't say that. Never say that,' she screamed. The power in her lungs surprised her and her mother was tamed. But then a large toothpaste bubble formed on Aisha's lips and burst.

The other children rose. A deep gloom filled the house. So Jaan went to the fridge to look for cucumber slices. Mother and Laila screamed at once, 'Get out.' The girl ran to the toilet. Mother started cooking without a word because it was time for school. Laila began to help in silence, as she normally did. The younger sisters wondered what they must do. They discussed a joke they could crack. Javed, who is fifteen, slipped out of the house. Even when things are normal, with so many women in the house he feels he is living inside a television serial. Aisha went to Laila and tried her luck. 'Don't go to Malegaon,' she said. Laila did not respond. She was looking prettier than ever. Her hair thicker than usual because it was wet, skin glowing, back so strong and straight. Just seeing her this way, Aisha was tortured by dark thoughts. She imagined this beautiful creature exploding.

'I don't know why I feel so scared today. Don't go so far away,' Aisha said.

'Shut up and get ready for school,' Laila snapped.

The house was calm when the children left, but Laila and Mother clearly were waiting for everyone to leave to resume the fight.

'My sister is a student and a businesswoman,' Aisha tells the class. 'She is one of the youngest businesswomen in the whole world.' For a moment she thinks there is applause, which Laila deserves. But it is merely a disturbance in one portion of the classroom. The girls near the window are excited. Someone screams, 'She is here. It's Laila, I think. She will live for a hundred years.'

Through the window, Aisha sees her sister walk into the school. She wonders if Laila has ever received applause. Has she ever stood on a stage and received the applause of the world? Do some heroes pass through their lives without ever seeing such a moment?

She knows nothing bad has happened. Laila was rude in the morning and she has come to hug. That is her way. Aisha asks the teacher if she can step out for a minute, and she runs down the corridor, down the stairs. On the grounds, Laila and Aisha run towards each other and burst out laughing because they know the scene is from some Hindi film, maybe all the Hindi films ever made. They hug.

'So you're not going to Malegaon with Jamal?' Aisha says.

'I am. I came to give you a hug because I didn't hug you in the morning. Now don't ask me not to go. That's inauspicious.'

'Are you really going to Malegaon?'

'Why would I lie?'

'You're not going to Gujarat?'

'Why would I lie about that?'

'You know all of us would go mad if you were going to that place.'

Laila did say a few days ago that she may make her first trip ever to Gujarat but when Aisha started hitting her with a rolled Urdu newspaper, which is very light, she promised she wouldn't go. If she ever went to Gujarat, Aisha threatened her that she would hide all her shoes and clothes. Laila has six pairs of shoes. She is a bit hip that way. Strictly speaking, Laila has thirty pairs of shoes, because all the shoes in the house were bought by her.

'Damodarbhai doesn't own Gujarat,' Laila says. 'There are millions of Muslims there and they are very happy. But, anyway, I am not going to Gujarat.'

'Mother says you're a very good liar. You always were, she says.'

'Now don't annoy me, Aisha. I'll be back tomorrow by evening and I'll ring the doorbell with my nose.'

'Why your nose?'

'Because I'll be carrying gifts in both my hands.'

They giggle.

Laila jogs on high flat heels towards the iron gates. She is so elegant. As she opens the gate, Aisha sees Jamal's little blue car waiting on the lane outside.

11

Around 2 p.m.

INSIDE THE RING of furniture around the tunnel's entrance, Akhila is with the Major and four senior officers from Mumbai Police. The cops, who look like suave businessmen in shirt and trousers, are very sure that the man in the debris is involved in terror. By 'terror' the cops mean Islamic terror. 'He is not a pioneering Buddhist terrorist?' Akhila says. The cops don't get the joke. There is a problem with their hypothesis though. Not a single Muslim lived in the fallen building. That is what the survivors say. The residents are puzzled by the inquiries of the police about Muslims in their chawl because they have not been told about the mumblings of the man in the hole. That is a secret, for now.

It had not occurred to Akhila to take his photograph. So the Major sent a soldier into the tunnel for that, but the residents are unable to identify the man probably because of the layers of dust and blood on his face and the poor quality of the flashlight photographs. Or, they have never seen him before.

The Major's plan is to intensify the rescue while keeping him alive and talking as long as possible. He has suspended the efforts to scrape the concrete beam that lies over the man's legs. It would take hours to break it. The plan now is to dig another tunnel that would lead to the place where the man's head rests. The soldiers would then pull him out through the second tunnel. Nobody knows how long that will take. Soon Akhila will crawl in again, stab him with saline, feed him, clean his face, take better photographs and check his pockets for ID. And, of course, gather everything he says. Only she can get close enough to hear him. If he becomes communicative, she will ask leading questions to establish his identity. There is something else that she considers doing but she does not plan to discuss it.

There is one obvious concern – how safe is it for her to slither over a delirious terrorist? Very safe considering his state, the men assure her, but they agree there is a small risk. One option is to send a soldier crawling behind her but then the soldier would only cut off precious air supply for both the dying man and her; and of what use would the soldier be anyway when she is being strangled in the tunnel. The passageway is so narrow he would never be able to get beside her. So, the Major gives her a knife.

'When you're in the hole with him,' the Major says, 'tell him his family is safe, his children are safe. It's not enough to feed him, we've to give him hope and good news. To keep him alive as long as possible, we need to ensure his mind does not wish to sleep. He may not rise.'

He hauls her by her waist as he does with men and takes her for a walk outside the ring of cordons. It is bizarre that there is something pure about this burly rustic man; she has never felt a man's waist hug that is so devoid of sexual meaning.

'When you first heard him say those things, how did you feel?'

'I think I just wanted to listen more.'

'Then?'

'Then I got spooked.'

'Anybody would be spooked. You were on top of a terrorist. Some kind of a terrorist.'

'When that struck me, I tried to flee and I bumped my helmet on the rocks, my legs got stuck, I was a bit of a mess. Then I calmed down. I looked at his face, I saw how pathetic his condition was, and I calmed down.'

The Major keeps nodding his head.

'Does he move his hands freely?' he asks in a whisper.

'He doesn't but that's because he has no space.'

'I don't want to scare you but we don't know who he is. Be very wary.'

'Yes.'

'When you get on top of him, keep the knife in your hand, pointed to his stomach. Don't let him see the knife.'

'It would be funny if I get attacked in there.'

'Not funny.'

He spots Abha wandering about and calls out to her. He takes a scribbling pad from his back pocket, tears a page and gives it to the little girl. 'We don't know if it's your father but if it is, would you like to draw something he would like?' He gives her his fountain pen. Abha gives the paper and pen back to the Major, who thinks the girl is rejecting his proposal. But she takes out a notebook from her bag and a black sketch pen, and begins to draw.

'Where did you find these?' he asks.

She does not respond. Without raising her head she asks a reasonable question.

'Don't you want me to draw something my mother will like?'

'Later,' the Major says.

Abha draws the image of a little girl with two parents on the beach.

'I'm sorry I've to fold it,' Akhila says as she carefully puts the sketch in her pocket. Four other girls come running. They ask Abha for pages from her notebook and sketch pens, and they begin to draw. 'It could be my father, not her father,' a girl says.

Abha goes to the debris and sits alone, on a concrete slab. A soldier gives her a bun, which she holds like a monkey, and eats. The sight of a little girl eating alone has always made Akhila crumble within. She wants to take the orphan away from all this to a very affluent hotel room – that is her idea of escape. Far from her mother's idea of escape, which was running away to the theatre sets of rich Indian Marxists: abject rustic poverty.

AKHILA WAS FOURTEEN when her mother died. The cause of death was cerebral malaria. *Plasmodium falciparum* is usually a class-conscious protozoa. It does not go near Indian women who read Camus, especially Marxist feminists. But Ma had taken to roaming in forests, real Indian forests that were probably as big as whole European nations.

Ma was born into wealth at a time when it must have been glorious to be rich in Mumbai. Childhood was happy, suspiciously royal. She grew into a sharp young woman in serious glasses with large frames. To wedding receptions she wore controversial backless blouses and saris tied lower than the national mean.

Many of her generation and class dug Marxism, though most of them needed heroin to go with it. Some of them, who are now reformed capitalists manufacturing steel pipes, rubber pipes, commodes and things one would not imagine someone actually mass-produces, come home even today to chat with Pa over cheese and wine. Much is said about Indian Marxists and their love for French wines when they wish to discuss poverty and revolution. Actually, they are happy with South African wines, too.

The friends laugh at the memories of 'those days' when they signed up for an armed rebellion. Three of them did get as deep as Ma but when the police captured them and started massaging their balls, they called their papas, who couriered the bribes, and that was pretty much the end of their revolution. They surrendered to the new money and made it more money. Now they laugh. Thousands of students who followed their lead, who had no rich daddies to call when they were captured, don't laugh because they do not exist. Many just vanished from police custody.

Pa was made of the same strand as her. His family sent him to England to study chartered accountancy. Instead, he returned a radical with plans to overthrow the Indian government.

They had met at a 'debate', by which Marxists mean a discussion where everyone is saying the same thing to people who have the same views. One day, he went to her home, fell on his knees in front of her parents and asked them for her hand. They married without ceremony and drove to his beautiful house by the sea in Worli. They did not wish to have a child. Akhila was an accident. Mother probably thought she would be able to pull off the rebel-and-mother act. Something like the goddess with many hands that no-talent men draw as a gracious compliment to womenfolk. But Mother could not find the many phantom arms. Father transformed. Poor man, he chose the boredom of a gentle affluent family life over revolution, but Mother was too deep in. She tried to sit at home but that was just not her way. She was always looking at the door. Not metaphorically. She felt so stuck, she really did keep looking at the door.

A beautiful woman whose eyes keep wandering to the door – that woman exists in almost all the moments of her daughter's severe memory of her. A woman in a vast sunlit home; a woman with long proud hair in love with her good-natured husband, the sort of man who, wherever he stands, makes his space the edge of the frame. There is laughter in that house, and long conversations; the woman bathes her girl, cuts her nails, buys her frocks, but those eyes, they are never still.

And there are those hugs, fierce hugs entangling mother and daughter, which mean Mother is leaving again – to do good in some miserable little factory town, or a village on the edge of a forest.

And the woman vanishes from the sunlit home, vanishes for days, weeks, but never months. And her presence is now somehow deeper. Akhila waits, that is what her childhood is mostly about – long waits. She waits on the steps, watching the end-of-days rains of Mumbai; she waits when she walks to school, in the class, and when she returns from school. Every single day when the girl returns from school she hopes to see an unfamiliar car in the porch, or the sound of happy guests, or the other signs of Ma's return. Most days, there is just the silent indestructible unchanging house.

And when Mother does return, the girl goes crazy. Pa, on the fringes, looks on fondly. There are, once again, fierce hugs. Mother cries only when she returns, never when she leaves. One other time she cried. When she had slept with her daughter and discovered in the morning that the girl had tied her hands to her mother with a skipping rope.

A few days later, Ma vanishes again. And the girl resumes her wait. As Akhila goes in the back seat of a long car, through the happy lanes of Mumbai, she sees other girls with their mothers, and she condemns the vulgarity of love. How can people flaunt such luxury in plain sight in a world where other girls wait for their mothers? It is worse than the vulgarity of rich little girls going in big long cars.

Akhila has 'active' grandmas, as the active grandmas say. The old women get along even though they do not understand the language of the other; maybe that is why they get along. They have to depend on English to communicate, which tires them. They smell of oils; Ma smells like a forest. Once, the girl gets typhoid. Ma, in a jungle, gets to know and she rushes back. But she is desperate to just go back. There is a lot of work to be done before the Indian government is overthrown and all poor people are transformed into not-poor-but-not-too-rich by some kind of communist magic.

Some chaps have started a new party, something that says 'Maoist'. The girl is sure they mean 'moist'. Perhaps all the newspapers got it wrong. After all, Ma and comrades work in a tropical forest, which is most certainly a rainforest. But Pa says the word is not 'moist'. Ma is a 'Maoist'.

'What is a Maoist?'

'Her boss is Mr Mao. He is Chinese. That's all you need to know.'

But the girl has a lot of questions. She figures that what Ma plans to do, as a Maoist, is tell hunters and farmers who live in forests and villages that they can become happier hunters and farmers if they win independence from India and if they chase away every private company that tries to give them a lot of money for their land. The girl begins to read about Mr Mao. In the first five minutes she is excited. He is dead. Mother's boss has been long dead. She runs to Father and says, 'Does Ma know?' Mother knows. The girl is confused, dejected. She had thought that if the news of Mr Mao's death is broken to Ma, she might shut up shop and return. But Ma knows. She works for a dead Chinese man. Right. The girl reads more about Mr Mao. She is even more confused. She figures that Mr Mao actually wanted farmers, at least most of them, to become factory workers. And he took away so much grain from farmers in China that millions of them starved to death. He seemed to have been a very cruel man. She runs to Pa. 'Mao was not a Maoist,' she says. 'Does Ma know?' Mother knows. Kind of. 'Mao's ideas were right,' Pa says. They just didn't turn out the way he wanted them to. Right.

Ma thinks she can make Mr Mao work better in India than Mr Mao could make himself work in China. But the Indian government thinks Maoists are enemies of the nation. It bans Ma's party. She does not quit. She goes underground. Akhila is now eleven. Father whispers, though nobody is in the room, 'Your mother is in hiding.' She is in hiding with a band of armed malnourished tribals whom she is preparing for a revolution. Madam has progressive sclerosis. She can barely write her own name any more, but she has started carrying a gun in the forest. That is what a messenger says.

The messenger is a sliver of a man with no legs. He comes home crawling on his powerful arms. In the living room he sees a giant map of India on the wall and gets agitated. He asks Pa for a red pen. 'Only red'. Akhila gives him her red sketch pen. The man asks Pa to carry him, which he does. The man begins to draw red circles on the map, scores of red circles until all of India is filled with red. 'The revolution is coming,' he says. Father, still carrying the messenger against his chest, looks nervously at the girl.

After the messenger is put on the floor, he tells a story about Ma. It is too late for Pa to send the girl inside, the man has begun his story and it is brief. There was a battle with cops in the forest. Malnourished tribals versus malnourished men in uniform. Mother, on the side of the malnourished tribals, lay behind a shrub and took aim, her finger shivering over the trigger because of the sclerosis. She did not shoot, he said. Somehow she escaped capture on that occasion.

The police in three states are looking for Ma. Akhila lives every moment in the fear that they will capture and torture that beautiful woman. Ma continues to come home, but not as often as before. And when she does, it is always in the cover of darkness. Then there are, once again, those fierce hugs. More than ever, Ma loves long steam baths and head massages given by her own mother.

Obviously, only the close family knows about her visits. On one of her visits, she is in a bad way. She has high fever. For security reasons she goes alone, in disguise, for a blood test. She goes to a cheap government hospital because she has accepted that she cannot be an honest Maoist if she continues to enjoy things only a lot of money can buy. She scribbles a phone number for the attendant to call with the results. But her sclerosis is so bad that her numbers are indecipherable to the attendant. He calls a wrong number. What he wants to tell her is that she probably has cerebral malaria and she has to be admitted immediately. Days pass.

She gets into such a bad state that she is unable to move. Father has had enough. He takes her to the best hospital in the city. But it is too late. In thirty hours she is dead, cremated, her ashes flung. The girl, now fourteen, needs to wait no more.

On one of her visits, Ma had given the girl a photograph. It is of Mother standing with a dozen tribal women. The girl has taken a particular dislike to the photograph for reasons she does not understand. One day, two months after her mother's death, the girl writes a caption on the back of the photograph. 'Cool Indian feminist with prospective maids'. The girl cries for hours.

Many of the factory workers, farmers and tribal hunters Mother tried to save were eventually saved by private corporations who either bought their land or employed them. They were saved by semi-literate merchants who had no intentions of doing good but who did more good in the way of making money than Ma ever did. That hurts.

Father does not wish to talk about all this. He is a merchant himself now who owns tea plantations in two states. But he is still a Marxist, he still says, 'Capitalism is dangerous, so much inequality, so much.'

One evening, as he sits watching the news about a violent revolt of a car factory's workers, he keeps making angry noises even as he sips his wine. Akhila can take it no more. 'Why don't you go live in Sweden?'

'I don't hate this place,' he says.

'You do. It whips you every day.'

'India is a wound,' he says in a professorial tone. He is a bit drunk. 'But it is not a wound like a whiplash. It is a wound, like a spouse.'

THE MAJOR HAS cleared the compound by spreading the lie that there has been a gas leak. That persuades everyone to leave the plot and join the large mob outside on the street. The journalists are happy to go. The story has no visuals, and no prospects.

Now there are just the soldiers, four police officers and Akhila left on the site. She sits on the ground and does some stretches. And she crawls into the tunnel with a small bag strung to her back. In the bag, apart from the medicines, is a knife.

The crawl is easier than before. She does not shut her eyes to endure the slither over the stiff hand, but she does not feel the groping this time. For a moment it is eerie but it occurs to her that a soldier must have stuffed it back into the debris.

The man's eyes are open and vacant. His pulse is better, feet not so cold. She is bringing him back. She shouts, 'Can you hear me? What's your name? If you can hear me, blink thrice.' There is no response. She gives him the saline infusion in the tibia. She hides the pocketknife in her palm and slithers over the beam and on to his body. She looks carefully into his eyes. They look without focus. 'Can you hear me?' He does not respond.

She wears a pair of surgical gloves and unzips his trousers. He does not react as she picks his flaccid penis as though it is a flower and inspects it. He begins to mumble, which startles her. She shoves the organ back into his trousers and slides over his upper body. She puts her ear to his mouth, and listens.

12

A Telephone Conversation

FOR A MAN who is ashamed, Professor Vaid looks a bit too comfortable in the coir armchair. But that has more to do with the nature of the armchair. He has just learnt that Miss Iyer was assaulted in the morning. She was slapped and kicked and punched by patriots, but the attack was brief. The Sangh uses simpletons well, but on days there is a price it pays. He has since made some calls. The girl is safe, at least for now. She would be wise to take down the video, and hide for a few days before she is forgotten. But it is unlikely that she will.

She has survived the attack well though. Despite the injuries, she has been crawling in and out of a tunnel all day, and feeding a dying man.

The old men of the Sangh would argue that such attacks are not entirely unnecessary. Fear is important. They have said that for decades. They are among those men who have not read Chanakya or Machiavelli but love the synopsis.

Vaid has forgotten his old confused opinions about crafty practicality. There was a time, he does remember, when he believed that the practical were people who were incapable of being artistes. But now that he knows many in the arts, he is not so sure.

He had joined the Sangh for very clear reasons. Because he rejected the West, everything about it except its exquisite science, and he rejected the new world order that required the modern to imitate white people. He felt a deep revulsion for the posh imitators who then ruled India. They were an unspeakable human disaster. Their socialism starved hundreds of millions to death. The living fared worse. In the end, the socialists said, sorry, there has been a mistake, someone had read the wrong book. What India had practised was not socialism in the first place, they said. Nobody on earth knows its name. Decades of trauma had ensured that Indians had even forgotten the simplicity of pride. Even in that they imitated the white man. They searched for spurious scientific and cultural achievements to be proud. Does a person truly need victories to feel proud of his home, of himself? Vaid joined the Sangh to save his people from all this, save them from the epidemic of cultural retardation.

He still has faith in everything that first led him to nationalism. But then faith is a form of fatigue. The tired body calling an end to ceaseless doubt, the body preserving itself through the myth of absolute certainty, isn't that what faith is in its very core? Isn't that what love is, and the final draft of a poem, and all of finished art? The body claiming, 'It's good,' when what it is really saying is, 'It's enough.' You stare long enough at the world, you see fatigue.

His phone rings. It's AK again.

'Professor, there is a girl.'

'A girl?'

'There is a girl, Professor, with Jamal. He picked her up along the way. That's what our friend in the debris is saying.'

'They are in a car?'

'Yes, they are in a car.'

'Where are they going?'

'We don't know, yet.'

'So the cops don't know where to look?'

'They are going mad. Now they know there is a couple carrying a parcel around but they don't know where to look. But there is something more interesting. The man in the debris says the "Bureau" knows.'

'By Bureau he means ... You're not saying...'

'The Intelligence Bureau. The IB knows about the movements of Jamal and the girl. That's what he means.'

'Did he say "Bureau" or "Intelligence Bureau"? Bureau can be a word for a sleeper cell?'

'I'll tell you how specific he is. He says, SIB knows. I've got an audio file of Akhila's recording. He says SIB.'

'That's State Intelligence Bureau?'

'No, it's Subsidiary Intelligence Bureau, but yes, it means the same thing. It's the state division of the Bureau. Not many people call the Bureau SIB.'

'And what did you mean by audio recording?'

'The cops asked Akhila to record the man's mumbles. They would need it later as evidence in court and for their own records.'

'She is fully cooperating, then.'

'No. She said she is not handing over her phone to anyone after this thing is over. She is clever. She knows that if she records him on her phone she will have to surrender it to the police or the court.'

'So how is she recording the man?'

'She is using a cop's phone.'

'Alright. What do we have here, AK? A Muslim couple is on the loose and the IB is on to them. But your friends in the Bureau are saying they have no idea what's going on.'

'Exactly.'

'Doesn't make sense at all.'

'I know. I'm in touch with the top guys. They won't hide anything from me. Not today.'

'True. They have to suck up to you.'

'The director of IB swears there is no operation under way.'

'Maybe the man in the debris only means to say he is afraid the Bureau might be shadowing the couple?'

'Possible, but his language is ... but then he is just a man who is not in his senses.'

'What else is he saying, AK?'

'He is saying, "Someone get the girl out of that car fast." He keeps saying that. The same thing over and over.'

'Get the girl out of the car?'

'Yes.'

'Why do you think he wants the girl to leave the car?'

'Maybe Jamal is going to blow up the car.'

'Why do you think our man is so concerned about the girl alone?'

'Maybe he likes her. Or, maybe she doesn't know what she has got into.'

13

Miss Laila, Armed and Dangerous

MUKUNDAN IS UNABLE to guess the nature of the relationship between Jamal and the girl. He is yet to see an indisputable sign of love in the blue Indica, like kissing, or a hand reaching out to squeeze flesh or a man throttling a woman. But then the Indica has been travelling at over eighty kilometres an hour, and it has not stopped or slowed down since it left Mumbra. Some lovers are careful on the highway, perhaps.

He has tried to gather some information about the girl from his friends without revealing that he is shadowing her at the moment. They had the tone a lot of people in the Bureau have when they speak to him. They talk down; they are affectionate, but they talk down because he has always made it very clear he is not as smart as they are. It is not entirely a lie. There is something about speech he has not fully mastered. He has thoughts of reasonably good quality but they do not emerge as speech. It is as though he is always forced to speak in a foreign tongue. Even to him he often sounds intellectually austere, like when brown cricketers are forced to speak in English during post-match press conferences. But he does not mind his handicap, which probably does not have a name, hence not considered a handicap. When people speak to him, they lower their guard, say things, a lot of things.

The world is filled with people who wish to impress when they speak. It is not a bad idea at all but there are advantages in being underestimated. That, too, is the art of conversation.

No one seems to have any clue about the girl. Mukundan has no doubt that Jamal and the girl are very familiar with each other. The only thing he is not sure about is whether they have met without clothes. Jamal does not have a sister. Maybe she is a cousin, a niece, or an employee.

If they are lovers, what is it that she sees in a man like Jamal, a married thirty-five-year-old man with kids who is stupid enough to be shadowed by the Bureau? What do women see in most men anyway? You look at girls laughing in the company of their men and you would think humour is a very common male talent, which it is not. Shouldn't love be the reward for the clever alone? The rest must receive only loyalty, which is a very different thing. But the world does not work that way. But then, to imagine love as high tribute is to fall for the historical lie of lovers. Love is probably a lower emotion than its reputation. That thought always comforts him.

He is the sort of man who, if he ever gets entrapped in love, would turn out to be a good eternal husband. He knows that, and he fears his own captivity. At a level of living it is smart to be a good husband because it is smart to be good. He understands morals as a system of logic. In most situations there is usually only one right path and millions of wrong turns.

And everyone, in a given era, in a given place, knows what is right. If you forget your time, if you forget your place, there will be trouble.

Maybe he is a bit naïve when it comes to women and sex. When his niece was born, after he saw her in the cradle, he could not masturbate for a whole week. Sex seemed like such a depraved act of violence. With the angelic face of his infant niece in his head, he even started having dreams about the general welfare of women. And in his waking hours attempted another poem. About a reporter with the *Malayala Manorama,* who has got the greatest journalistic scoop of the century. He has stumbled upon a stunning secret that is eventually headlined, 'All Lost and Stolen Girls in the History of Humanity Revealed to Have Been Forced into Stenography'. The story has an extraordinary impact on society, especially fathers, who lose their fears. They release their girls from their hawkish vigil. Girls suddenly find the freedom to roam their towns, like boys, and they begin to thrive.

Mukundan has worked hard many nights on the poem, but the words just won't come.

AS USUALLY HAPPENS to a discreetly pursued car, the blue hatchback begins to assume bleak human qualities. It looks stupid, debased and tragic, its haste comical because it is only racing towards a carefully laid-out trap. A little blue car duped by the republic, a young intelligence officer on its tail. How did these fools get into this situation when life is actually somewhat beautiful, and easy too, no matter what writers say?

He has always found the shared tragedy of a couple heartbreaking. Something particularly sorrowful about the togetherness of man and woman in misfortune, even if they are not lovers. He would not want to look at their faces when their destruction begins, in a few hours.

He wonders why the Bureau has planned to capture Jamal this way. Why not just pluck him at home, or when he goes to the market? There would be too many witnesses? And, maybe they want to take him with his supplies, whatever it is that he is carrying in that bag or in the boot of the car. Also, Boss wants to know if he is going to pick up any interesting characters along the way. Apart from a young woman, that is. Men, dangerous men, that is what the Bureau is looking for.

Mukundan hopes a miracle will occur, that the Indica will stop on the highway and the girl will get away. She is probably only getting a ride to the home of a relative, who lives in one of those gloomy grey buildings by the highway.

The phone rings in his shirt pocket. It is Boss. 'Sir.'

'Is the girl still there?'

'Yes, sir.'

'We have to extract her before we take the car.'

'Sir.'

'We have about five hours to do that, if they don't stop anywhere. But we can't have a situation where Jamal changes his plan.'

'Sir.'

'We just want the girl out of the car, that's all. Nothing else should change. We want him to be on course, we want him to come to us. We're waiting.'

'Sir.'

'But we don't want the girl.'

'Got it, sir.'

'We extract the girl without Jamal changing his plan.'

'Sir.'

'If you have a plan let me know. Don't intervene until then. If things change, call.'

'Sir.'

'The thing is, Jamal might collect more people along the way. We are interested in those people.'

'Jamal threw his luggage in the back seat, sir.'

'So?'

'He is not expecting anyone in the back seat, sir. Or maybe there are a lot of things in the boot, sir.'

'Let's wait for a while, let's see if any men board. And then take a call.'

'Sir.'

'I'll be in touch.'

'Sir.'

'We have to extract that girl.'

Mukundan can see why the presence of the girl is a problem. The Bureau wishes to take Jamal to a safe house, get all the juice out of him, or flip him into an informer. What use are terrorists in prison? The Bureau can abduct shady men and keep them in illegal detention for months until they are of no use. Then they are handed over to formal custody. Sometimes they die. The Bureau is allowed to get away with that because there are things a nation must do. But it would be messy to abduct a young woman who is probably just another girl in the company of the wrong man in the wrong place. If she were to be left in the car, she would be a witness to the abduction. If she were to be abducted, she would have to be seriously implicated in terror or eliminated because illegal confinement of a woman is not the same as that of a man. There would be hell to pay. And if the abduction does not go smoothly and there is a gun battle, a dead young Muslim girl would draw too much attention.

Mukundan knows what the Boss is thinking – if the girl is in the car when Jamal is abducted, she is going down with him. The Bosses would have no choice. That, or call off the operation. But the Bosses are not the sort of men who would call off an operation just to be fair to a girl.

What is required is that Laila just vanishes from the car. Actually, that is not a good summary of his assignment. If she disappears into thin air, Jamal would be baffled by the magic and he might cry 'Allah-o-Akbar' and abort his journey. What is required is that Laila leaves the car according to the laws of physics, and Jamal still carries on. What must Mukundan do?

His mind grows quieter. Outside, the world is ugly and prosperous. Giant factories stand where there used to be green fields. The air is grey and people are in the spells of purpose. He has entered Gujarat. Damodarbhai country. A land of merchants where artistes are rare, at least among men.

14

Laila

EVERYONE IN THE class probably saw the blue car. It is good for Aisha's reputation if people know her sister travels by car some days. She wishes they also got to know that the man in the car was once a Hindu Brahmin who converted to Islam. That is even better than white people converting to Islam because white people are like Brahmins to black and yellow and brown people, but white people who convert to Islam are usually just crazy. But the Brahmins, they are never crazy. As in a doctor would never say they are crazy. They always know what they are doing and they are very clever. But that is all Aisha wishes the class to know about Jamal. The rest of him is not so nice. At least what her mother says about him is not.

A week ago, after dinner, when she and Laila went for a walk on the terrace, Aisha had asked what exactly Jamal did. They went in small circles, watching the ocean of lights that surrounded them. On a clear day, they can see the lights of Mumbai. They love the city, the crush of people and the shine of the rich.

'He does many things,' Laila said. 'Like me.' And she chuckled fondly at some faraway memory as though he was a shop window in Mumbai.

'Like what?'

'He lays cable. And he is working on starting a perfume business. And many other things. Do you know what satphones are?'

'Sounds familiar.'

'Liar.'

'They really do.'

'Satphones are satellite phones.'

'I know.'

'You don't need a SIM card for them.'

'I know.'

'But they are banned because cops won't be able to trace calls made on satphones. So he has been trying to get the government to let him bring some satphones here.'

'Legally?'

'Yes, legally.'

'Why?'

'He says some fat businessmen want satphones. He is helping them with permission and stuff like that.'

'I hope it's not something shady.'

'Everything is a bit shady in our country. You can't do anything straight.'

'You don't go with him when he is about to do something shady.'

'I won't.'

'Does he really beat up people?'

Laila laughed, but she nodded.

Mother Taliban has discouraged Laila from being seen in public with him ('People have mouths'), but Laila does what she feels like. Jamal has dropped her home a few times and when something like that happens in Rashid Complex at least a thousand people get to know. At all times there are people in balconies, behind windows, on terraces and on the ground too. Once, when Laila was walking Aisha back home from school, as she does sometimes, a funny thought occurred to her and she made Aisha take out her protractor. They held the protractor at arm's length and found people in every angle, except angles 80 to 110.

There is much talk in Rashid Complex about Jamal and Laila even though there is an official story about the two. It is a sort of story that begins with the deathbed scene.

Aisha is suspicious of deathbed stories because it is all very convenient that the main character is dead. The story is that two years ago, when their father was dying slowly in the general ward after the accident, he called Jamal to his side. He was apparently his business partner. And appointed him Laila's father, and asked him to pay for her college education. So Jamal is Laila's guardian. Aisha wants to believe that because it is sweet, and safe. But it is not a very convincing story. She had never seen Jamal until a few months ago. And nobody remembers the deathbed scene except for Mother. Also, the story appears to have become public knowledge only a few months ago.

Laila refuses to talk about Jamal and she pretends to get angry when her sisters try to dig.

Aisha wonders why a devout bearded Muslim man, however wonderful and kind, would ask a much younger man to be the father of a pretty teenager. That's creepy and there are things that even men know are creepy.

Mother probably invented the story so that people don't sneer at Laila. This guardian business is exactly the kind of half-baked story that she would tell.

15

Damodarbhai

THE MAN IN the saffron loincloth carries a large vat up the stairs. It is heavy, filled with copies of the Koran in Urdu, Arabic and English, whatever he could lay his hands on. He places the vat on the terrace and surveys the low skyline of Faridabad. In all those homes people know that a new emperor has come to rule, a beautiful glowing man with a silver beard and a fifty-six-inch chest; a man who closely resembles the most famous of Mohanjo Daro relics – the sculpture known to informed people as 'Bearded Man'. The emperor is a prophecy of the great ancient Hindus. He is half-history-half-biology, that is what Damodarbhai is.

Among the copies of the Koran in the vat is a small bottle of kerosene, which he empties over the books. He throws a light and watches the books burn. An intense joy fills him as the books, tortured and helpless, are deformed. He begins to chant the name of the emperor as he has done every week in the past five years. 'DaMo, DaMo, DaMo.'

The man in the loincloth is an insignificant lawyer, he does not deny that. He is one of the defeated men who stand in black costume outside a court to solicit work. Every evening, on his way back home, he buys copies of the Koran. He steals them when he can. Never in his life has he stolen anything else.

It is not easy for him to hold that book. He has to quickly put it in a bag. What an object to touch. He has always hated Muslims, those untrustworthy reptilian men; those meek women in burkhas; those boys who go to madrasas, the way they look at women who are not inside a shroud; and that sick green of their culture; the diabolic medieval mosques of the psychotic conquerors from Arabia; and the Saudi-sponsored mosques and the nasal whine that comes from within. Wherever those wretched people are, in whichever corner of the world, there is trouble. That's their nature, their training. For centuries, they butchered Hindus. In every riot, they butchered Hindus. It stopped twelve years ago, in 2002, when Damodarbhai showed them, finally, to whom the nation belongs. He has now come to rule all of Bharat.

The lawyer got the idea of burning the Koran when a librarian in Jaipur was arrested for doing that. The librarian argued in court that the Koran was a regressive and dangerous book. If Indians are allowed to burn copies of the Indian Constitution, why must they not have the right to burn the Koran? The man was sentenced to a year in prison for hurting the feelings of Muslims.

The enraged lawyer filed a petition demanding the right of Hindus to burn the Koran. The court threw his petition out. That evening he bought a copy of the Koran, went home, tore a page and burnt it in the kitchen, ignoring the questions of his wife, who had long acquired the habit of looking puzzled every time she saw him. He kept tearing pages and burning them. He felt an immense joy, a cosmic joy. In the days that followed, he began burning whole copies. But one evening he almost gutted the kitchen. After that incident he started going to the terrace. One day, as he was burning the copies, he was impelled by a higher force to remove all his clothes. When the neighbours, from other roofs, objected, he went back home and wore a langot. The neighbours never wondered what he was burning. The morons only see the dick of a man, not what he is about, what he wants, how he thinks, what he does.

He has invented a ritual, that is what he has done. The fire in the vat grows, the books are now almost ashes. Matter that was trapped in medieval madness has been liberated.

16

A Telephone Conversation

IN THE FRONT, beside the driver, there is a bodyguard with an automatic gun. It is not clear to Professor Vaid how one boy with a gun would be of any use when Islamic terrorists come to kill him, as they have promised several times. A pilot van of unarmed police is ahead. The farcical dwarf cavalcade of two vehicles moves at a brisk speed.

The roads even in Nashik are good these days, at least half of them are. There are straight white median markings too. How swanky all this is. The nation was once a village and order, any kind of order, was considered a form of arrogance. Many years ago, he saw three half-naked workers painting a series of white lines on a highway. They had all the right tools but the lines were crooked. For miles. He asked them why they were drawing crooked lines. 'We are not ruled by white bastards any more,' one man said. 'Why should the lines be straight?'

Are Indians innately a crooked-line settlement that has been infected by a straight-line civilization?

Vaid is on his way to the Mumbai airport, which is five hours away. In Delhi, he has a string of events including a lecture on

'How the Left Steals Compassion, Fiction and the Wound'. Before his lecture, a woman in her thirties or forties, she would know the difference, will walk to the podium in a spectacular sari and say several flattering things about him, all of them true. He will begin his lecture with his usual words. 'I'm too old to lie', which is a lie in the first place. Then he will say the same things he has been saying for decades but in different words:

'Activism is always a feudal system in which nobodies are in the care of somebodies. It begins in a special moment when the elite of a system become the underclass in another system.

'Intelligent women, for instance, in a system controlled by men. Affluent or talented blacks in a system of whites. High-caste Indians in America, rich Third-World Muslims in the West. Writers in Indian languages in a nation where English-language writers are culturally dominant. They are all elites of one system who become the underclass in another system. There are more. The progeny of old money, in an age where crass new money has overtaken them and made real estate too expensive for them. Mere millionaires in a system of multi-millionaires. Mere multi-millionaires in a system of billionaires. Billionaires, too, in a system of highly intelligent machines whom they defame because they have no one else to fear. Gandhi, the affluent upper-class racist, in a system of whites who once denied him entry into a first-class train compartment. Ambedkar, who too was denied entry into a first-class compartment, an elite low caste, in a system of Brahmins. It appears that if only passenger trains were equitable systems, many revolutions would not have occurred.

'When the elite of a system become the underclass in another system, they search for a moral cause to restore balance of power.

This is popularly known as activism. Upon finding the moral cause, the elite co-opt, enlist and employ naïve simpletons to fight the battle. Activism is always a retaliation of the elite, always couched in morals and always a feudal system where the strong employ the weak, the poor, the demented, the suicidal, the semi-literate and other losers of the society.'

It may not be wise to mention that the Sangh, too, is a form of activism.

After the lecture, he will meet Damodarbhai, who does not pretend to touch the feet of elders any more. That is a relief. As a fat man his plumbing does not permit a full bend, so he bows, throws a hand in the direction of the elder's crotch and touches his own chest.

AK will be present at the meeting. He has been calling with detailed information about the man in the debris. The event is minor by AK's standards but the fact that intelligence should flow from a man trapped in the rubble of a fallen building in the heart of Mumbai would naturally fascinate him. AK is a scholar of anomalies. Miss Akhila Iyer will find him amusing if she ever gets to meet him.

What she would see at first glance is a plain little man in oversized shirt and trousers, with a flat forgettable face, narrow eyes behind thick spectacles and black hair parted sideways as though he is in a bad disguise. Not many ordinary citizens know of him, but Miss Iyer is an informed woman, she may have heard of him. If she has not, she will in the coming weeks, when Damodarbhai makes him National Security Advisor. Reporters will then tell, once again, his spectacular back story with no attributions at all because the source is AK himself.

The legends of men are the proof that they tend to overestimate the beauty of their own lies. What else can explain their lame fables when they could have spun almost anything about themselves? Young Fidel Castro was tried out for an American baseball team. Mullah Omar stitched his own eye after it was destroyed by shrapnel, and he sprang from the bed singing a Persian song. What's wrong with these men? Is it so hard to tell a fascinating lie? The legend of Damodarbhai is duller. The best he could invent of his past was that in his youth he had gone off the grid and wandered for three years. That is almost a plagiarism of Jesus Christ.

The legend of AK, on the other hand, is extraordinary and it has endured for years as a settled truth. It does help the myth that he was an intelligence officer, and that about nine years ago he had retired as the most decorated director of the Intelligence Bureau, a position he held for just a year.

The story is that he spent seven years undercover in Pakistan, and in that period, in the summer of 1988, he slipped into India as a Pakistani spy and infiltrated a ring of Indian terrorists holed up in the Golden Temple. In this period he was also a negotiator when Indian planes were hijacked, often the lead negotiator. In fact, from 1971 to 1999, he was a negotiator during all the fifteen hijackings of Indian airliners.

There is probably a lot of truth in these stories. The Patriarch has worked with him closely. The man is not a sham. Three years ago, together they influenced a retired semi-literate army truck driver, who used to whip drunkards in his village, to go to Delhi, sit on a pavement and go on a fast-unto-death in protest against the corrupt government of the Gandhi dynasty. It was televised as a revolution, an Indian Spring. So the revolution followed. Thousands began to gather around the old man – first the poor, then the richer. Bankers carried their children on their shoulders and pointed to the old man far away. That is what good fathers do when they feel they are within a historic photograph – they carry their children, especially daughters, on their shoulders.

AK was then warming up for the elections. He was not the only patriot working to achieve the end but the only one whom all the squabbling patriots of Sangh adore. Some men are like that – even though they are alphas, everyone likes them. He even convinced the stingy old patriarchs to part with the money to build a right-wing think tank. Not all patriarchs knew what a think tank was, but his involvement assured them that it was something conspiratorial.

AK calls again.

'Professor.'

'Yes.'

'Not a single Muslim lived in that building. That's what the residents say.'

'Then he is an outsider, a friend. A very, very unlucky visitor.'

'Possible. Our Akhila Iyer wiped his face as much as possible to clear the blood and dust, and she took a clear picture but the residents are not able to identify him. But then his face is still covered with layers of things. I've got an image on my phone.'

'Alright.'

'Professor.'

'I'm here.'

'There is another matter.'

'What is it?'

'He is not circumcised.'

'What did you say? Did you say circumcised?'

'He is not circumcised.'

'How do you know that?'

'Akhila Iyer. She goes into the tunnel, unzips the dying man and checks his penis.'

The men fall silent for a while, then they burst out laughing like adolescents.

'If he is not a Muslim, who are we dealing with, AK?'

'Some of my police friends who have seen naked Muslim men in custody tell me that now and then they do see a devout Muslim who is not circumcised. So our man could still be a Muslim.'

'So late in my life I learn something new.'

'This girl. She is something.'

'You may have done a background check on her by now.'

'Yes. I understand that you're acquainted with her, Professor.'

'Your sources are impressive, AK.'

'Our patriots beat her up this morning.'

'I know.'

'But they didn't hurt her much.'

'I know.'

'What do you think of her, Professor?'

'I don't know her. I've only seen her pranks.'

'I feel you're thinking what I am thinking.'

'What am I thinking, AK?'

'You're wondering if the whole talking-man-in-the-debris thing is a prank.'

'No, no, no. That's what you think.'

'These are the facts. There is certainly a man in the hole. Half a dozen soldiers have taken turns to go into the tunnel. So we know he exists. We have his images. And we know he is mumbling things. But only the girl can hear him because only she can get so close to him.'

'You told me she has been asked to record the conversations.'

'She is doing that. But what if she is fabricating the faint voice of a man. That's not hard.'

'She crawls into the tunnel and makes up a voice? Do you believe your own theory, AK?'

'Not entirely. But why are you so sure it is not a prank.'

'It's not her style. She is not the kind to use a dying man for a prank. She is a modern young woman, AK. They are all ethical. And what's the prank anyway?'

'Making asses out of the entire intelligence and police network.'

'But she has to record the facial expressions of the people who are being pranked. That is the whole point of her pranks.'

'Maybe she is doing that.'

'But the people who are being pranked, AK, is us and the police officers who are searching for Jamal. She can't shoot those faces.'

'Do you remember Aradhana Shanbaug?'

'That name. It's so familiar.'

'The classy commie who went into the jungle to start a revolution.'

'Yes, yes, yes. She died. Didn't she die?'

'Akhila Iyer is her daughter.'

'I see, I see. Alright.'

'This girl is not normal.'

'She is not. Of course, she is not.'

'What stops her from attempting a prank in any situation? Maybe she will follow it up for several days. She will get her facial expressions then. She has a lot to play with.'

'This girl, AK, her pranks are not just fun. She has a motive.'

'She, too? Don't people do anything for love any more?'

Vaid laughs more than he thought he would.

'What's her motive, Professor?'

'She wants to show a world where the heroes of the left are useless.'

'She sounds like us.'

'She does. AK, before you go, what else is our man in the debris saying?'

'He is saying that Jamal and the girl will soon go to a restaurant, but we don't know anything about the restaurant.'

'Nothing about where they are right now?'

'Nothing.'

'Jamal is meeting people in the restaurant, you think?'

'Maybe. The curious thing about our man is that he has been talking only about the girl. He says almost nothing about Jamal.'

'But he has not given her name yet?'

'No. He takes Jamal's name but not the girl's.'

'What's he saying about the girl?'

'"Ask her to run away from the restaurant." The same thing over and over again. If she stays with Jamal, the cops are going to kill her. That's what he says.'

'Cops?'

'Yes. According to him, the cops know where Jamal is going. They are waiting. The plan is to execute him.'

'That sounds like cops.'

'If the girl is with him, she goes too.'

17

Miss Laila, Armed and Dangerous

IN HOW MANY ways can a girl be extracted from a car without changing the mission of the driver? What if Mukundan's car bumps into the Indica in such a way that Laila is only mildly injured? In this country an accident is as natural as any act of god. But it is hard to choreograph a controlled accident. She might be seriously injured. Jamal, too. Actually, Mukundan, too. And this is not the type of plan Boss would clear. If Laila is injured in the accident, there is no guarantee that Jamal would put her in a hospital and continue on course. He may abort his mission. The same reason why Mukundan cannot risk mugging or assaulting her on the highway to inspire her to go home. If any of his actions make Jamal alter his plan, Mukundan will have botched up the whole operation. There are many things about the operation he does not know, including its real objective which might not be as simple as abducting a terror suspect.

An elegant way of extracting Laila, and he is an admirer of elegance, is to administer an injury to the girl's parents in Mumbra or her siblings, if she has any. This can be carried out through a burglary or a street incident. Laila would then have a good reason to rush back home, leaving Jamal to complete his mission alone. But the Bureau would take time to collect information about her family. All they have is the description he has given them and the place where she was picked up by Jamal. The Bureau must have already started digging around but they have to be very careful. If they tap the wrong kinds of informers, the operation would collapse. The slightest slip would warn Jamal that the Bureau is on their tail. It is unlikely that her family can be used in the next few hours. Even if that plan can be executed, the Bureau would be counting on her family contacting her. At this moment it is not clear whether the girl is carrying a mobile phone. He has not seen her with the device. And the information is that Jamal's phone is still dead as it has been since dawn.

There is a development. The blue hatchback finally slows down and drives into the parking lot of a highway restaurant.

18

Laila

THE CLASS IS drawing the 'political map of India'; the geography teacher is sitting in a trance, her eyes baffled and frozen, a finger picking her nose as though someone has asked her to do it at gunpoint.

It occurs to Aisha that India looks like an ice-cream cone, including the thumb of an unseen child who is holding the ice-cream. The thumb is where Damodarbhai comes from. As she draws the bulge of Gujarat, she feels as though she is drawing the contours of a hostile foreign land, like Pakistan.

She marks major cities on the map. Malegaon is too small to qualify, but she marks it anyway – north-east of Mumbai, not very far from Gujarat. Aisha Raza hereby recognizes you, sweet Malegaon, with a red dot. She doodles a line between Mumbai and Malegaon, a windy line to make it look realistic. Laila is somewhere on that route. Unless she was lying. What if she is actually headed to Gujarat? Aisha feels a familiar gloom in her lungs. Malegaon is safe, it is in Maharashtra and it is filled with Muslims.

Aisha has been to Malegaon. Laila took her last month. They went as Naaz's chastity guardians. Naaz is old, almost thirty, but she and Laila are good friends. It is not clear how, but even though Laila is only nineteen, she knows a lot of fully grown women and most of them have jobs that are very odd. When Aisha asked what her friend does, Laila said, 'When the hero and heroine fall in love, Aisha, you know they start dreaming about being with dozens of extras in the background, who dance in formations? Naaz is one of those dancing girls in the background.'

One Sunday, Laila took Aisha to a film set in Goregaon, which is about an hour from home. The set was a giant shed. They were early and the dancers were just trickling in. They would arrive in salwar-kameez, go behind a narrow door and emerge in shiny golden miniskirts and sleeveless tops. Their bodies glistened. 'It's mustard oil,' Laila said. 'Inside that room, some spot-boys apply mustard oil on them.'

'Why mustard oil?'

'I don't know why mustard oil. What I know is those spot-boys must be running to the toilet often.'

'Why?'

Laila laughed but did not explain.

Most of the dancers had big thighs and paunches, but Naaz was not so bad. She, too, arrived in salwar-kameez. The sisters were in a far corner, on a bench. Naaz made a gesture to suggest that she would talk to them later. She went into the mysterious room behind the narrow door and after ten minutes emerged with almost nothing on, but she was wearing short cycling shorts under the skirt. She, too, was glistening.

'Does her family watch Hindi movies?' Aisha asked.

'Her family knows what she does. She feeds them, so they shut up. That's all there is to this family-trauma business. You feed them and they shut up. By the way, this is not a Hindi film.'

'No?'

'It's a Marathi film. Hindi films are now for rich people and brown folks who live in America and Britain. They don't want girls like Naaz any more. She looks too poor. These days all the dancers in Hindi films are hip girls.'

'If we were dancers, would the producers think we look cheap? But we're fair.'

'What's the big deal about being hip? If you speak English and say "fuck" five times in every sentence, you become hip.'

'You know that's not it. It's our faces. There is something about our faces that is not very English-English.'

'Not you. You look expensive, Aisha.'

'You too.'

'We are trendy girls.'

'Very trendy girls. Flashy, flashy.'

'Do you see that some of the girls are not wearing cycling shorts?'

'Yes.'

'They get twice as much as the ones who are wearing cycling shorts.'

'Because they are not so shy?'

'It's called "special rate". There is a special rate for not wearing cycling shorts. And there is something called "V-cut special rate". That's for the swimming pool dance sequence. If you agree to wear a bikini, you get V-cut special rate.'

'Why V?'

'That's the shape of the bikini bottom, you silly girl.'

The dancers stand in formation and when a man screams 'one two three four', they begin. In this sequence there are no leads, just an arrangement of extras dancing, kicking their legs in tandem, punching the air, flapping their knees, juggling their breasts. It looks like a very difficult way to make money.

After the shot, Naaz brings three cups of hot tea.

'Save me, Laila. I am going out of business,' she says.

'You have Marathi films. Won't you survive?'

'Films nowadays are becoming realistic.'

'What do you mean realistic?'

'No song-and-dance. No dream sequence. Grim stuff.'

On the way back home, in the auto, Laila was quiet. She probably felt sorry for her friend. Aisha kept talking without a break but Laila's mind was probably still on the film set. When Aisha tired of talking, which is rare, they travelled in silence. There was something sad about the silence. Then Laila said, perhaps to herself, 'Wherever we go we meet only losers, we only meet people who barely survive their miserable lives. That's why I like Jamal.'

It was the first time she had mentioned Jamal without any prodding.

'Why do you like him?'

'He is not a loser. He does stuff. He makes money. He is the only person in the world who can help me. Everyone else I help. He gives me work.'

'What work?'

'This and that. I work as a receptionist for him some days, I do a bit of accounting, some sourcing.'

Laila may grumble about her loser friends but she is a good friend. A week after meeting Naaz on the sets, she fixed up something for her.

In Malegaon, a bunch of Muslim boys have started making spoofs of Bollywood and Hollywood classics. Some of those spoofs, which are played in small video halls in a dozen towns, run for weeks. Laila got to know that they were going to shoot *Malegaon Ka James Bond*, and through some friends she somehow managed to contact the director on the phone and convinced him to cast Naaz in the lead. She sent him her photographs. Laila can be very persuasive. She even got her a fee of ten thousand rupees for a two-day shoot. Naaz was ecstatic but she said she would go only if Laila accompanied her. That was how the three of them set out to Malegaon in an AC bus, the tickets paid for by the producer of *Malegaon Ka James Bond*.

Malegaon turned out to be a filthy, congested weavers' town lined with dark tiny looms from where scrawny sullen men looked at young women on the street as though they were a funny joke they didn't fully understand. All the young men had hairstyles with middle partitions. The town looked a lot like Mumbra. Black slush on the streets, green puddles, giant pigs, herds of goats going somewhere, the smell of decay in the air and several little mosques.

'I hope everyone here is not Muslim,' Aisha said as the three girls walked from the bus stand to the hotel.

'Only half the population is Muslim,' Laila said. 'Why do you hope that?'

'Or people would think only Muslims are filthy.'

Laila giggled but it was her unhappy giggle. She said, 'Last year when I was walking back home, I saw a crowd of Muslim men around a roadside barber's radio and they were listening to something. I got curious because there was so much pain in the faces of the men as they listened. What was on the radio? It was Damodarbhai's speech. Some men laughed, made faces, mimicked Damodarbhai, but they could not conceal the pain. I've heard the speech only three other times, but I remember every word of the first minute of the speech. Every word of it as though it is a great poem.'

Aisha, too, now knows the speech.

Friends, why are Muslims so filthy? Filth is disorder. What is disorder? Disorder is the rejection of order. It is not merely the rejection of beauty, of hygiene, of the law; filth is a deliberate rejection of the state. The filth and chaos of Muslim streets, my friends, is the rejection of everything we hold dear. We know this because once we, too, sought refuge in chaos. When the Mughals invaded us, broke our beautiful temples and destroyed our way of life, we withdrew into filth and ugliness. That was how we waged our war. That is how we protested. When the British invaded us, broke our beautiful temples and destroyed our way of life, we withdrew into ugliness because to accept the beauty of the invader is to be co-opted by them. We know that. We understand organized chaos because we invented it. But today we have begun to invent our own beauty and order. But the Muslims reject that. That's why they are filthy. They are filthy because they reject us, they are filthy because they reject India.

'What a horrible man,' Naaz said.

Aisha threw glances around to check if any of Damodarbhai's devouts had heard her. It is simple things like this that get people hacked on the street.

The reception of the Majestic Hotel was disappointing. It was her first time in a hotel and she had imagined that it would be opulent. But still it looked better than home. There was a man waiting for them. His T-shirt was torn at the armpits. He probably didn't know. 'I am Farook,' he told Naaz. 'I am the director of *Malegaon Ka James Bond*. It's our great fortune to receive a party from Bollywood. You look more beautiful than in your pictures. Your friends, too, but I've never seen their photographs.' He said he was a tile-polisher and a poet. So many poets these days. He, too, had a hairstyle with a middle partition. 'You girls have nothing to worry at all,' he said. 'We treat women from Bollywood with utmost respect, offer them only mineral water and send them back with their honour intact.'

'Can you show us our rooms?' Laila said.

'We have booked only one room because of budget constraints. But it is big enough for three of you.'

'AC?'

'There are only non-AC rooms in this hotel.'

'I hope you have brought the cash,' Laila said. 'Hundred per cent upfront.'

He looked hurt, but he handed an envelope to her, which she passed on to Naaz. Naaz was worse than Laila. She started counting the cash. Farook stood there and recited an Urdu couplet about trust, money and love.

A short man wearing sunglasses walked in. The bellboy asked him for an autograph, which the short man in sunglasses obliged. 'He is Malegaon's Shah Rukh Khan,' Farook said. 'Doesn't he look exactly like Shah Rukh Khan?' A few minutes later, Malegaon's Aamir Khan walked in. Then Malegaon's Amitabh Bachchan, and Malegaon's Will Smith, who was dark and had curly hair. All of them wore sunglasses. Over the next one hour trickled in malnourished welders, weavers and tile-polishers, who were all lookalikes of famous men. Then a small and very frail man appeared in a black suit. He was Malegaon's James Bond. 'I wore the suit in honour of our guests from Bollywood.'

'This is his debut film,' Farook said. 'He is a welder when he is not an actor.'

On his index finger was a ring that let out red and blue lights as though he carried his work in his ring.

Early morning, Farook came to fetch his female lead. Laila and Aisha went along. They walked to a playground where a crowd of spectators had assembled. James Bond, in his suit, was watching some activity around a bullock-cart. A man was tying a small video camera to the yoke of the cart. The ox was grazing a hundred metres away. The excitement in the crowd escalated when they saw Naaz and Laila walk towards them. Farook told the crowd, 'If I hear one disrespectful word about our guests from Bollywood, I'll turn into a monster.' That made Laila giggle. She probably liked him a bit. But she would never ever have a crush on a man whose T-shirt is torn.

The crew was going to shoot all the scenes involving Naaz in the film over the next two days. In the shot that they were setting up, Naaz would be abducted by four goons and James Bond would rescue her. Malegaon's Bond is very scared of fighting goons, crossing the road and swimming. He ends up rescuing people by chance. When Farook said 'action', James Bond began to run. A mob of spectators pushed down the rear end of the bullock-cart hoisting the cameraman sitting in front, on the crosspiece. Bond grew tired after running just twenty metres and stopped. It was not clear whether it was part of the act or the little frail man just could not run.

A day later, after all the scenes involving Naaz were canned, 'the Bollywood party' went back to Mumbra. A week after their return, Laila said that the shoot of *Malegaon Ka James Bond* had been suspended. The financier of the film, a lineman who worked for the electricity board, had thrown in a sudden demand: he wanted his son to be Bond.

'So why didn't the director agree?' Aisha asked.

Laila didn't know why. But she found out a few days later. Malegaon's puny Bond had lung cancer and he was dying. He probably had just a few weeks to live. It was not a secret apparently. Death is never a secret among the poor. Starring in the film was the greatest thing Bond had ever done in his life, and the tile-polisher director did not wish to replace him even if that meant losing the film.

'Maybe you should call James Bond and chat with him,' Aisha said. 'He liked you. He was tongue-tied when he would talk to you.'

Laila looked lost. She was very affected by the news. 'It would cost just fifty thousand rupees to make that film.'

'That's it? That's like five small TVs.'

Laila said she would convince Jamal to invest in the film.

'He will do that for you?' Aisha asked.

That annoyed Laila. 'This is not a favour,' she said. 'He can actually make money from producing Malegaon's films. This is business.'

Jamal sent the cash, the film was completed. A few weeks later, the director sent a CD of the film that also had a five-minute video of the première night when the entire local crew had assembled to watch the film. James Bond arrived on a cot in his black suit, holding a toy gun. He was too weak to walk. His cot was carried by the crew from his home through the narrow alleys of Malegaon. Great crowds cheered him all the way to a small video hall. He looked so happy, a puny, frail, happy dying man. Six hours after the première, he died. He was twenty-five.

After watching the film, which was horrible, and the footage of James Bond's journey to the première, Laila and Aisha went for their usual walk on the terrace.

'Spoofs, all spoofs,' Laila said. 'Everything that the poor do are spoofs. Welding, tile-polishing, weaving, hawking, running a tiny store, fixing bikes, taking calls, and every single thing I do, every single thing Father did – these are just spoofs of the big games of big people.'

19

Damodarbhai

SOMEWHERE IN A colony in Gurgaon where the per capita income is higher than Britain's, a plump fourteen-year-old boy sets out to play tennis. A scrawny dark maid is carrying his tennis kitbag, which probably weighs half as much as her. He walks free, a metre ahead of her. He cannot bear to see the sight of the mule swaying under the burden though the kitbag looks particularly expensive on her.

The boy is in a good mood. Everybody at home is in a good mood. A new government is coming. Father was dancing when he was watching the election results. 'God,' Father said many times, 'Damodarbhai is my God. Our God.' The boy has not seen his father so happy in the past five years. The Gandhi dynasty has ruined the nation. Father's chemical import business has almost sunk. And they have been unable to sell any of their six flats in Gurgaon. The family had to cancel its annual European holiday for three successive years. They went to Malaysia, instead. Malaysia. What next – Thailand? Father says the Gandhi dynasty has also made low-caste people talk back to those who feed them. His factory is full of them, so he knows. And they have become expensive, too. That is because of 'the socialism of the Gandhi dynasty', Father says. 'The employment guarantee scheme for lazy farmers is making these bastards bold.'

The mule who is carrying his tennis racquets has been talking back. Last week she said she wouldn't wash the family's underwear any more. 'You wash your things yourself,' the woman told Mother, 'I won't wash yours. And I won't wash the panties of your daughter. She's not a kid any more.' The maid said 'panties' in English. Father got upset when he heard that sister wore panties. The boy agrees there is something very vulgar and sexual about the word 'panties'. Father ran out of his room, clenched his fists and screamed at the maid, 'Never ever say that my daughter wears panties.'

20

A Patriarch's Review

THE HIGHWAY TO Mumbai passes through vast flatlands. Professor Vaid gapes at the rice and millet farms, which look glorious and self-important, but they are only waiting for the day when they will become real estate. The village romantics, who usually live in the cities, cannot bear the thought. The romantics wish everything to remain the same because it is aesthetic that way.

Miss Iyer has harmed several village romantics, chiefly in a set of pranks called the 'Nobel Series' in which she fools the pious socialists into believing that they have been chosen for the peace Nobel. It is fascinating to see how the nice chaps behave when they are told they have won the good-behaviour award.

For one of the pranks she deploys three white men and two white women, all of them middle-aged tourists she had collected from a cheap hostel in Colaba. She takes them to meet P. Sathya, whose malady of interest is rural affairs. He is a serious humanitarian with an accidentally fashionable hairstyle. Like every philosophical thug of Miss Iyer, he despises large corporations, agriculture reforms, land reforms, biotechnology, and the fact that rich men wish to acquire land. He wants small farmers to remain small farmers, half-naked in their tiny hamlets. He has, of course, won the Magsaysay.

Sathya is alone in his office when Miss Iyer herds the foreigners in. She has concealed a tiny high-resolution camera in her spy-bag, which has an aperture for the camera's lens. Sathya's assistant, a thin, excessively reverential man, ushers them in and leaves the room. Sathya is gracious. He is under the impression that a group of professors from a Norwegian university wishes to meet him to understand the traumas of Indian farmers. He is good with traumas, he loves traumas.

'We have been a bit disingenuous,' Miss Iyer's voice says with an accent that she wishes to pass off as Scandinavian. 'We are not from a university. This is an unfortunate custom we need to follow in our line of work.'

'I don't understand,' Sathya says, still gracious.

'We are in reality from a committee set up by the Norwegian Parliament. I am just a regional facilitator. I live in Oslo but I was born here, in Mumbai. These are not the members of the committee, but representatives of the members.'

Sathya looks bewildered but he is an informed man. A great but elegant excitement begins to descend on him.

'Mr Sathya, we are from the Norwegian Nobel Committee,' a solemn man says.

Sathya, still pretending that he does not know what is going on, throws a glance at the window, at a distant time, as though in quiet reflection of his whole life.

'Mr Sathya,' a woman says, 'the Norwegian Parliament and the Norwegian Nobel Committee are honoured to confer the

2014 Nobel Peace Prize on you for your lifelong dedication to the welfare of Indian farmers.'

Two remarkable things occur. Sathya believes them at once. It is as though he always carried in his heart the hope or conviction that this moment would arrive. The other remarkable event is that he begins to cry. Upon receiving news of an extraordinary recognition, the selfless weep in joy, inadvertently revealing the impossibility of selflessness.

The woman requests Sathya not to break the news to anyone until four hours later when an official statement would be issued from Oslo.

'In about four hours, the working day in Oslo will begin,' Miss Iyer says. 'We will convey the news to the world then. We just wanted to meet you to confirm that you accept the award.'

'I accept,' Sathya says, wiping his eyes with a kerchief, 'I accept.'

The reason why Miss Iyer met him so early was probably to ensure that the real Nobel Committee would not be in a position to deny the news if Sathya leaked it in his excitement. After all, he has been a journalist for decades and has close friends in the profession.

The prank has a second part, which is its core. She sets up a Skype appointment with him, claiming that the Nobel Committee, sitting in Oslo, will formally break the news to him.

Four hours later, the Skype interview begins. Sathya's face, which has acquired extreme compassion, appears on the screen.

'Yes, I'm here,' he says. 'But I can't see any of you. I think your video is off.'

'That's unfortunate,' the voice of Miss Iyer says. 'The whole committee is present, they can see you from Oslo. The group who met you today in your office, sir, we are in a conference room at the Taj Hotel. We can see you, too.'

'Hello,' Sathya says meekly, wondering what he must say to invisible influential Norwegians. 'Hello, Committee.'

'Something has come up, sir,' Miss Iyer says with reverence. 'There is an issue, sir.'

'What issue, ma'am?'

'You're a propagator of a concept called "farmer suicide".'

'What do you mean by "propagator", ma'am?'

'You've propagated the idea that Indian farmers commit suicide because they are in debt.'

'I've not propagated anything, ma'am, I've been ...'

'But several studies have disproved this. It appears that Indian farmers commit suicide for the same reason why many millionaires commit suicide: they are suicidal, they are depressed. It's a mental health issue, it appears to us, not a debt issue.'

'What is it that ...'

'Maybe poverty is one of the many factors that push the depressed to take extreme steps.'

'I don't see how this ...'

'In fact, if we look at the matter statistically, sir, poor Indians in the agricultural industry are least likely, I repeat least likely, to kill themselves than richer Indians or even South Koreans in general or Australian farmers in particular.'

'Ma'am, there is a ...'

'Also, if you're portraying farmer suicides in economic and

sociological terms, what explains the fact that the number of male farmers who commit suicide is many times higher than female farmers, who are the most oppressed creatures on earth? The skewed ratio, sir, matches perfectly with a global phenomenon of depression-induced suicides where the number of men who accomplish suicide is many times higher than women.'

'Ma'am, what are you trying to say?'

'There is a concern that you have created the myth of farmer suicide to milk it for your activism like other fucker-doodle-do-gooders.'

'Excuse me?'

'And why did you cry when we told you that we are giving you the Nobel. You want it much?'

'What's going on? What the hell is going on?'

'You sound angry, sir.'

'What the hell is going on?'

'Sir, this call may be recorded for quality and training purposes.'

'What?'

'This call may be recorded for quality and training purposes.'

'Is this some sick prank, you semi-literate corporate bitch …'

'No Nobel for you.'

Sathya's lips tremble. He looks to his left, and to his right. Some words escape his mouth but it is not clear what he says. As Miss Iyer would put it, we are unable to follow his dialect any more.

21

Miss Laila, Armed and Dangerous

IS SHE AN accomplice? What if they are in this together? Mukundan asks that question only because he needs to. He knows there is no way he can find an answer by just sitting in his car and observing her.

The sun has lit the breeze. It is as though someone is holding a hairdryer to his face. He has parked the WagonR on the shoulder of the highway, about two hundred metres ahead of the entrance to the restaurant complex. He has a clear view of the Indica in the massive parking lot, which is largely vacant. Jamal and the girl step out. She covers her head with her dupatta and walks with brisk steps, her young slim figure defining her kurta.

All she has to do is keep walking, without a word, away from the parking lot, keep walking away from that man and not return to his car, that is all she has to do to reclaim her life. Or, if they are lovers, they should have a fight like good lovers. She must ask him to abandon his wife and children, and surrender to evil pussy; and he must blurt out that she is not so important to him; then she must start crying, she must give him a tight slap, and he must slap her back like a true Malayalee; and she must walk away to a bus stand. All she needs is the luck of a bad day.

He is tired of his focus on the girl, tired of his compassion, which has been fierce for the past several hours. His compassion is not a farce but there is an honest question he has asked himself many times in his career: How does he endure such extraordinary miseries of people that he witnesses almost every day in his work life? And that, of course, leads to many unspeakable questions. He does not have a clear view of himself but he has seen the glint of evil many times in other men, very noble men. Activists and doctors and poets, who are in the proximity of human pain because they wish to be that close and watch. Do people really believe that sadists live alone in a dark room? He can take you where sadists are more likely to be found – in the very places where the miserable come for relief.

After about an hour, which is a very long break, he sees the couple walking back to the car. They appear to be having a conversation. When she speaks, only her head moves. Maybe that is the way she speaks, or it is because she is carrying plastic bags in both her hands? Jamal, too, is carrying such packets. It appears that they are carrying water bottles, meals and snacks. When they reach the car, Laila opens the back door and throws the bags on the back seat. Jamal does the same. The luggage that he had flung on the back seat when he left home is still there. If he was going to pick up some dangerous men, he would have put all those bags in the boot. It is possible that the boot is filled with interesting objects, but still, the way things are being dumped in the back suggests that the car is not collecting more humans any time soon. This, of course, is not a clinching argument. But if Boss is waiting to act until he is certain that Jamal is not going to pick up more friends, it is probably a waste of precious time.

Mukundan feels that the next time Laila takes a toilet break, a team of just three officers will be able to abduct Jamal in his own car. The girl will return from the toilet; she will be perplexed by the missing car and, of course, the missing man. She will be confused and angry, but safe.

As the blue hatchback moves down the parking lot, Mukundan loses sight of the car behind the concrete guardroom. A few seconds later he sees it in his rear-view as it merges into the highway traffic. As the Indica goes past him, he catches a glimpse of Laila. She is looking ahead and talking with an amused face as a wind blows her hair. All the windows are open. She takes off her dupatta and throws it on the back seat.

22

Laila

AS A MEMORY, Rashid Complex is always a grey place, which is strange because there are a million shades of colour here; there are colours on a single clothesline that even girls would not be able to name. Only the buildings are gloomy, and their little dark windows. Yet, as a memory of a place, at least in Aisha's head, it is grey. Like you remember some creative women in cotton saris as women with large bindis, while in reality they wear small dots.

She is walking home, lugging her schoolbag down the broken roads that no one ever repairs. The street is filled with people and vehicles and cows and asses and pigs, the pavements are filthy as always and there is the smell of sorrow in the air; it is probably only rotting vegetables. She is a bit hurt that Laila did not tell her about her trip with Jamal. She likes the idea of Laila confiding in her but the fact is she never does. She could have told Aisha about the trip last night when they lay chatting.

It was a weird chat. The room was dark and everybody seemed to be asleep, even their mother who sometimes only pretends. Laila was, as she usually is when she is chatting into the night, lying with her head resting on her palm. Aisha was right next to her, the precious place. At some point, Laila fell silent, which was not unusual. That's how all of them go to sleep. They would be talking one moment and the next moment someone drops off. But after a long silence, Aisha heard her say something in English – 'radicalized'.

'Are you dreaming?' Aisha said.

'Yesterday some very wise men on the TV were debating the very deep question – why are there not so many Indian Muslims who are "radicalized".'

'What do they mean?'

'Why are Indian Muslims not going around planting bombs? That's what they mean.'

'What a dumb question.'

'How many people in a million should become terrorists for a community to be considered radicalized? Nobody knows. But what they want to know is why Indian Muslims are not radicalized. It's like a sweet surprise.'

Aisha giggled. Laila was being mean to wise men and that is always fun. 'One white scholar said Indian Muslims are kind of nice because of the culture of India.' Laila was now mimicking the white man's English. 'India is a multi-cultural, multi-ethnic…'

'Multi-grain.'

'India is this, India is that. That's why Indian Muslims are not terrorists. One man said, Indian Muslims have remained poor, and they have remained very religious, and their children study in madrasas but still they are not terrorists. How sweet, he seemed to say. How sweet.'

Aisha toyed with Laila's feet with her own. She wanted to see Laila's toenails, which are always bright red, but the room was too dark for that.

When Aisha gets home she finds a crowd of sisters, one lanky brother, one large mother who is cooking in the tiny kitchen, and two neighbours. The moment Mother sees her, she says, 'Your beloved sister has left her mobile phone behind.'

'Has she called?'

'Not a single call. Not one call.'

'You think she has forgotten our landline number?'

'That girl has the memory of an elephant. But elephant calves, they so love their mothers.'

'Now don't say anything mean about Laila.'

It is not like Laila to forget her mobile. Maybe she wanted to be left alone for a day. Too many needy siblings who call all the time. Aisha toys with Laila's phone. At first she plays some games, then she does the inevitable. She reads all her text messages. But they are very boring – about work, meetings and accounting.

Home is gloomy without Laila, or the prospect of her appearing at any moment. But that leaves her stuff unguarded. What are Laila's things, apart from the clothes and the footwear? The question has never occurred to Aisha before. In the corner of the only cupboard in the house are some notebooks that belong to her. Aisha goes through them. There are lots of lists, which are probably things-to-do written over several months. The children feature often. 'Buy slippers for Jaan; Javed's trousers are short.' In a corner of one of the notebooks Aisha finds a line in Hindi, which looks like a line from a poem:

'Sweetheart, we lurk like thieves in a world better than us.'

She does not understand what the line means. It is, despite its adult abstraction, the saddest line Aisha has ever read.

23

Miss Laila, Armed and Dangerous

THE LIGHT ON the highway is faint and it is not easy any more to spot the small car, which is somewhere in the swarm of taillights. Yet, Mukundan has given a big lead to Jamal, about two hundred metres. He expects the Indica to stop any moment. It has been a very hot day and Jamal is a man who respects water; he has been drinking constantly from a bottle. The girl does not drink so much probably because she wishes to hold off a trip to a public toilet. Their consumption of water is of interest to the Bureau. There has been a development.

Boss finally moved. He has sent five Bureau men. They are right behind Mukundan, in a white Sumo. They are armed.

They had broken away from the welcome party that had assembled at the trap, which is now only about eighty kilometres down the highway. Mukundan has less than two hours left to rescue the girl.

The Sumo men were waiting for Mukundan at a petrol pump. It was immediately clear to him that they did not have a concrete plan except that the objective now is not to extract the girl but to extract Jamal. The Sumo men and Mukundan will trail the Indica and if a clear opportunity arises they would pluck him when she is outside the car, and drive him away to the safe house. But if such an opportunity does not arise, they will not force it.

There is bad news for the girl though. For Jamal, too, who was doomed anyway, but the nature of his doom now looks bleaker than before.

Mukundan was under the impression that the abduction of Jamal was entirely a Bureau operation. But in fact it was always a joint operation between the Bureau and the Beard Squad, the gang of psychotics in Ahmedabad's Crime Branch. Officially they are called the Anti-Terrorism Squad but every cop in the region knows them as the Beards or the Beard Squad. They capture to kill. In the past four months they have eliminated twelve men, all of them Indian citizens, all Muslims and all of whom were apparently plotting to kill Damodarbhai. Across the nation there have been so many plots to kill him. It's as though killing him is the new Mecca.

Some people think that the Beard Squad is called so because they hunt Muslim men. But the truth is that 'Beard Squad' is a tribute to the beards who run it. Their ringleader, Bhim, colours his visible hair, including a full beard, red. 'Muslims should not exist,' he once said on television. He later clarified during a press conference, in-between chuckles, that he only meant all Muslims should convert to Hinduism, 'their true religion before their ancestors were raped by the Mughals'. This man carries a gun. But he, too, is a poet.

Bhim reports to the second most powerful man in Gujarat, whose Intelligence Bureau code is 'Black Beard', a bald cylindrical strategist on a high-sugar diet, once a biochemist, and now a minister in Damodarbhai's cabinet whose days begin early because he needs to get back home early. His mother does not go to sleep until she sees him. Some days he lies on a swing with his head resting on her lap, and he says the most beautiful things a son can tell his mother. On days, when he is this way, he speaks to Bhim on the phone. With his head resting on his mother's lap he gives clear, clever instructions, at times conveying a black warrant, settling the fate of some miserable scrawny Muslim. He is the only human in the world whom Damodarbhai trusts and perhaps even likes.

If nothing changes in the next two hours, Jamal and the girl will be in the illegal custody of the Beard Squad.

The Sumo men explain the mystery behind why Boss took so long to act. Boss has been trying to convince Bhim that the girl has to be extracted and set free, but Bhim wants the girl along with Jamal. Boss argued that she can be investigated later, but Red Beard would not listen. The two bosses had a big fight. According to Boss, the illegal detention of a young woman, who is probably a teenager, would be problematic. According to Bhim, the illegal detention of any Muslim is never really a problem.

The battle over the girl is in reality yet another squabble in the world between a practical man who has shame and a practical man who is not afraid of shame. The Bureau is like the good who appear to be good because they are terrified of being perceived as bad. The Beard Squad has no such fears. In fact, they are so lousy at covering up their murders that Mukundan suspects they want the world to know they are killers.

Things are going to get very ugly between the Bureau and the Beard Squad because the Beards are unaware of this side-operation that is under way to get the girl out of the mess. The Bureau is going solo. The operation, if it goes well, would have Jamal in the bag and a very confused girl on the highway, and some raging mad Beards.

FINALLY, THE PAIR of taillights shifts to the shoulder of the highway. Jamal's Indica slows down and stops on the edge of the road. Mukundan's WagonR swerves and comes to a slow halt. He turns off the headlights. Behind him, the Sumo, too, goes dark. In the lights of the passing cars, the Indica, which is about a hundred metres away, appears and fades.

Nothing happens for several seconds. The parking lights blink but the car is still dark inside. After a minute the driver's door opens and Jamal gets out. He stretches and yawns. He walks down the rough unpaved wayside in Mukundan's direction. He walks at least thirty metres.

Jamal is a decent man, at least while urinating. He has ensured that he is at a reasonable distance from the girl, about ten seconds away from his car, ten seconds of brisk walk. In daylight he would have been clearly in her line of vision, but not in this darkness. The highway is noisy and even if he screams she may not hear. Also, he has probably consumed so much water he would be peeing for at least a minute.

'This is it,' Mukundan says into the phone. 'Move.'

'I'm not so sure this is our chance,' a man in the Sumo says.

'This is,' Mukundan says and drives ahead with his lights off. He goes past Jamal and stops behind the blinking Indica. That gets Jamal's attention. Even as he urinates, he keeps an eye on the mysterious vehicle that has stopped behind his car.

'She can see him,' the man in the Sumo says. 'If we take him, she would know it was an abduction.'

'No, she can't see him,' Mukundan says. 'It's too dark. From where I am I can't see him at all.'

'She can see in the headlights of the passing vehicles.'

'She is not looking. She will not look at a pissing man. She is a young Muslim girl from Mumbra.'

'But if she wants to she can see.'

'She won't look. And she can't see him, trust me. And she won't look at a man who has his dick in his hand. She definitely can't now.'

Mukundan turns on his headlights. There is no way the girl can see anything behind her except the harsh lights. The lights may worry her but she is not going to step out of the car on a highway. As he expected, she rolls up her window.

Jamal wonders what is going on but he is not finished yet.

'Go for him,' Mukundan says as he gets out of the car. He walks to the roadside, phone in one hand and pretends to pee. That should comfort Jamal, who finally looks away.

'Move now,' Mukundan says. 'What are you doing?'

'Boss said, smooth. Smooth or nothing. This is not smooth. We're not sure this is going to be smooth.'

All that the men in the Sumo have to do is get behind Jamal, put a gun to his ass, gag his mouth and pull him inside. And leave. It would be over in five seconds.

'No,' the Sumo says. They won't budge.

Jamal zips up and begins to walk back to his car.

Mukundan gets back into his car and drives away. He gets a passing glimpse of the girl's dark figure. She is sitting tense, her arms folded, her large eyes follow the mysterious WagonR.

24

Damodarbhai

THE VILLAGE CHILDREN roar when the fifty-metre-long cracker begins to explode. A disoriented camel shits. The local Gau Rakshak Sena has sponsored the cracker in tribute to the victory of Damodarbhai. The cow protection force has only five official members. The chief is a thirty-year-old man with smashed ears, his cartilages destroyed by years of wrestling. When the fireworks end, he feels incomplete, as he feared. He is happy, even emotional, but he wishes there were more to the day. It has been eight years since he sold his land to the builders. He does not have to work any more, work ever.

He has the habit of asking himself very clear questions. 'And what would satisfy you?' He always finds clear answers. 'If someone does something wrong, if someone goes out of line, and if I can punish him.'

He begins to call his friends in other villages asking if there have been any movements of trucks. Over the past two years, as the patriots ascended, Muslims have been careful not to transport cows to slaughter during the day. They do it in great secrecy in the night. The locations of the slaughterhouses are widely known but the cops, those whores, they don't allow any trouble at the slaughterhouses any more. But they don't mind it if there is trouble in other places, far from the slaughterhouses. In fact, sometimes they help with useful tips.

About an hour later, he gets information about a truck passing through a dirt track about thirty kilometres from his village. Some bastards are taking the goddesses to slaughter on a day the patriots have shown to whom the nation belongs.

He collects a dozen friends in his Fortuner. It is not long before they intercept the truck. There are four Muslim boys in the truck and a dozen old cows. Gau Rakshak Sena liberates the cows, who amble away. The four Muslim boys stand with folded palms, begging to be spared. The men take the boys to a cowshed and tie them up to pillars. They bring hockey sticks from the Fortuner and thrash the buttocks of the boys, who wail. One of the men records the punishment on his phone. This is going to be a hit on YouTube. It may even get Damodarbhai's attention.

25

A Telephone Conversation

'PROFESSOR.'

'AK.'

'Have you reached the airport?'

'Not yet. But I've entered Mumbai, but I don't know what that means. It's been all concrete for hours.'

'I have news.'

'Go on.'

'The Bureau is still clueless about Jamal.'

'Alright.'

'They tell me they have no operation under way. They are not chasing any Jamal.'

'Do you believe them?'

'They won't lie to me, Professor. I'll screw them later, they know that.'

'So what's going on then?'

'There is something we are missing. Our man has been saying some interesting things. The cops who are lying in wait for Jamal and the girl, they are the Beard Squad.'

'He said "Beard Squad" specifically?'

'Yes.'

'So Jamal and the girl are going to Gujarat?'

'They are probably already there. He says the Beard Squad is going to execute the girl.'

'And Jamal?'

'He doesn't say much about him. But he says the girl is going to make a telephone call from a telephone booth.'

'How does he know that?'

'Exactly. I don't know.'

'At what time will she make the call?'

'We don't know that.'

'Are telephone booths still around?'

'A few. "Last chance", our man says. He keeps saying that over and over again. "Last chance".'

'Last chance for what?'

'To save her perhaps. When she is in the telephone booth, that's the last chance to save her. I think that's what he means.'

'Haven't they managed to chop the beam on his legs.'

'Slipped my mind to tell you. They are not going to chop off the beam. They are building another tunnel to pull him out head first.'

'How long is that going to take?'

'I don't know.'

26

Miss Laila, Armed and Dangerous

MUKUNDAN HAD ANTICIPATED the fuel stop but for the development to become an opportunity, a string of simple events needs to occur in the next few minutes. If Jamal leaves the petrol station a free man, he will reach the Beard Squad trap near Vasad Tollbooth in about thirty minutes, with the girl. Then it's over.

As Mukundan's car and the Sumo wait on the shoulder of the highway, just ahead of the petrol station, there are dense streams of vehicles lumbering on. The petrol station is tiny and rustic even though Ahmedabad is not very far. Here, there are only two operable tanks – one for petrol and the other for diesel. And there are two unequal queues of patient vehicles. The petrol line is short and brisk but the diesel line is long, and slow, because of the trucks. The Indica is in the diesel queue. It waits behind a water tanker, a truck and a red Omni van. There are several vehicles behind the Indica, which presents a complication. The car is effectively stranded in the queue. If the girl goes to the restroom, leaving Jamal alone, Mukundan can take over the vehicle but he would not be able to quit the line immediately because there is no space to turn around. The Indica has to wait for the vehicles in front to finish fuelling.

The squat office of the station is set a few metres away from the fuel tanks. On its wall is a large sign that says 'PCO. Calls within India, and international'. At the bottom of the sign is the word 'Toilet' and a long red arrow. The toilets are probably located somewhere behind the office, a thirty-second walk perhaps from the Indica. 'Make her want to pee,' Mukundan implores the gods. It is a reasonable prayer because she has not had an opportunity to take a toilet break for hours. But then he is not so sure if she must set out immediately. It will take Jamal at least ten minutes to refuel. If she leaves the car now, she will return before he refills the tank.

The water tanker that was fuelling heads out and a giant truck moves up the line to take its place. The red Omni van inches ahead, followed by the Indica, and the whole queue, which is steadily getting longer and has extended into the highway, moves a few metres.

He begins to feel that the girl has decided to control her bladder. Maybe she is terrified of public toilets, especially in a tiny, dim place that appears to be the haunt of truck drivers. Or, maybe she is debating the matter in her head.

The giant truck leaves, it is now the turn of the red Omni van, which should not take too long. Next up is the blue Indica in which there is some movement.

The passenger door opens and the girl steps out. She opens the rear door, grabs her dupatta and walks to the office booth. There she talks to an attendant, probably asking for firm directions to the toilet. She disappears behind the building. She is gone. Mukundan's phone rings. The Sumo is excited.

Jamal is finally alone in the car.

He is yawning as he waits for the red van in front of him to move. It would not be wise for the men in the Sumo to take him now even if Jamal co-operates and comes quietly. Too many eyes. A man in the queue to refuel deserting his idling car and leaving in the company of four burly men would be too conspicuous. Also, what becomes of the car? If it is abandoned in the queue, there would be chaos. It would probably be a bomb scare. There would be too much attention.

'We've to wait for Jamal to finish fuelling,' Mukundan says.

'The girl will return by that time,' Sumo's ringleader says.

'We have to delay the girl.'

The attendant shuts the fuel tank of the Omni van and the driver gives a wad of notes into his hands. And waits for the change. And waits. Finally, he leaves. The Indica moves up. As the attendant opens the fuel tank and thrusts the nozzle into it, Jamal steps out and stretches. All through the journey, Jamal has never been shifty, he has never looked at the world around him with even a hint of fear or suspicion, except once perhaps, when he was urinating on the wayside. The refuelling takes a while, he is probably tanking up. He thinks he is going a long way from here. He is, in a way, but not as he planned.

The girl may appear any moment. Mukundan gets out of his car and heads in the direction of the toilet. If he meets her on the way, he will pretend to be an acquaintance. Every man knows enough about a girl for a brief forgettable chat. That would delay her by at least a minute, maybe more. Before he can reach the office booth, he sees the attendant removing the nozzle from the fuel tank. Jamal gets into the car and drives around the fuel pumps. And he parks by the side of the station's exit. He is still within the premises of the station, but on the very edge. The way he is parked, the car will be in full view of the girl when she emerges from the toilet, which is probably not more than fifty metres away.

Mukundan walks to the Indica. All four windows are open. Jamal, who is sweating, is drumming the steering wheel and does not notice Mukundan standing at the door.

'Can you move your car, sir?' he says.

'What happened?' Jamal says. His voice is deep and strong, and he speaks with respect that almost feels like kindness.

'A huge fuel tanker is coming, sir, and we are clearing the way.'

'I'll take just a minute,' Jamal says. 'My friend has gone to the toilet. She will be back any minute.'

Mukundan scans the man. There is no sign of firearms on his body. He looks harmless, which he probably is not. The back seat has his luggage and water bottles. And a new Spider-Man toy in its case.

'I'm only following the orders of my boss, sir. The tanker is going to enter from here. It will be reversing and it will stand exactly here. It is so huge, I can't tell you. I think it is so big it might float on water. You can park right there,' Mukundan says, leading him into the shoulder of the highway. 'You see that white Sumo, sir? You see that WagonR in front of the Sumo? You park right there, just in front of the WagonR. You'll be fine. The cops don't mind.'

'Cops,' Jamal says and laughs. 'They don't mind anything.'

Jamal peeps through the window and surveys the driveway behind him, looking for the girl. He shakes his head and chuckles, probably at the whole history of women who have taken too long to return from the bathroom. And he drives out of the petrol station and into the shoulder of the highway. He passes the Sumo and the WagonR, and parks in the spot Mukundan has recommended.

Moments after the Indica leaves the petrol station, Mukundan sees the girl. She walks down a narrow path from the toilet. She does not look for the car. She heads to the squat office and enters a phone booth. This is perfect.

Mukundan marches towards the Indica. As he passes the Sumo to his left, he does not stop or even throw a glance at the vehicle. Those men know what to do.

He is going to fling open Jamal's door, show him his service revolver, which would persuade him to crawl over to the back seat. In that time, the four men from the Sumo will enter the Indica and flank Jamal. Mukundan will drive. Jamal abducted, the girl left on the highway.

Mukundan is only metres away from the Indica. He hears the Sumo's doors opening behind him.

27

Laila

MOTHER HAS BEEN muttering all evening. Often, she looks at the telephone on the stool and sends a rebuke. The sun has long gone down, but Laila has not called.

Laila had strictly asked Mother not to ever call Jamal on his mobile phone, but she could not help it. She called, but his phone is switched off. Maybe there is something wrong with his phone. He has probably dropped it in coffee, or Laila would have called from his phone. But even if his phone is dead, there would be so many telephone booths on the highway. Aisha concedes that it is a bit mean of Laila not to call. What must Mother do? She is on the floor, her legs stretched, watching TV. Aisha and her three younger sisters are in various places of the room staring at the TV, but no one is really following the story.

It is not easy for Mother to rise but she has done it a dozen times in the past thirty minutes. She goes once again to the phone, lifts the receiver and quickly puts it down. She has been checking if the phone is working. Aisha feels that Laila must be dialling home exactly when Mother lifts the receiver.

When Mother slowly returns to the floor, the phone, finally, rings. The girls charge.

Aisha is the first to reach it.

'Aisha, my angel,' Laila says.

'What took you so long?'

'I just didn't have the chance, my lovely doll.'

'Have you eaten?'

Mother snatches the receiver and screams, 'Couldn't you call?'

Aisha can hear the faint voice of Laila say, 'I just called, didn't I?'

'Why so late?'

'Should I be calling home every hour?'

'Have you reached Nashik?'

There is a pause, just for a moment, and Aisha's heart sinks.

'Yes,' Laila says. That's a lie, Aisha knows.

'I hear Gujarati. Some people in the background are speaking in Gujarati,' Mother says. 'Why do I hear Gujarati in Nashik?'

'Don't drive me mad.'

Mother asks a dozen questions about useless things – about where she kept the electricity bill, whether the telephone bill has been paid, whether the school fees have been paid. It occurs to Aisha for the first time that Laila and Mother have nothing at all to talk about.

Aisha has been spot-jogging, waiting for her turn to speak to Laila. For a moment she tries to understand the scene in the house. Three excited girls standing in line behind mother-hen waiting for a chance to speak to a nineteen-year-old girl, who takes care of all of them. Aisha is not sure if this is a happy moment or sad.

28

Damodarbhai

THE LIGHTS GO off in the banquet hall, there is a hush, then applause as a beam of light appears. Bill Gates, in a black suit, looks as though the spotlight is hurting his eyes, but that is just how he looks.

Against the receding ovation, he says, 'Thank you, thank you, I'm delighted to be here in Delhi. I thank all of you on behalf of the Bill and Melinda Gates Foundation.' From there he gets duller.

When he ends his short speech, there is more applause, and all the lights in the banquet hall come on. He begins to walk down the room towards the other end. His audience parts along the middle and makes an aisle for him. 'So biblical,' he mutters, but nobody gets it.

A flock of bright bridal saris flank him and he poses for pictures, holding the waists of two of them, but he is disorientated for a moment when he suspects they might be men. He realizes they are eunuchs whom his own Foundation funds to survive those who are not eunuchs. When he resumes his walk, he looks a moment longer than he needs to at every woman who greets him. He stops often as people extend a hand towards him and state with deliberate clarity a name, organization and a project.

'I'm working on portable diagnostic tool for waterborne diseases.'

'That's so lovely.'

'I'm working on a one-dollar phone.'

'Keep in touch.'

'I've made a paper microscope.'

'I thought that's already in the market.'

As Gates glides along the NGO guard of honour, the line of selfless inventors ends and a longer file of fieldworkers begins. They introduce themselves as maladies. 'Malaria'; 'Dengue'; 'Malnutrition in girls'.

Soon the parted audience merges and he floats to a corner escorted by friends. There is wine and murmurs. As is his habit, he catches words in the air and searches for a pattern, a dominant theme. It is all about Damodarbhai, naturally. They hate him here. The man is going to make it very hard for NGOs to get foreign funding. That's what everyone is talking about. Damodarbhai wants to break the back of the social sector. At various times, he has described the type of people in this room as 'frauds, misery miners, misfits in a talented world, fronts of Christian evangelists, CIA's donkeys'. What he wishes to destroy is left activism, but he is not going to make it look that obvious. He would have a go at everyone who receives alms from white people.

Hopefully, Damodarbhai would make a distinction between dubious trust funds of deceased capitalists, like the

Ford Foundation, and the responsible philanthropy of live capitalists. Gates looks fiercely at his wine glass. He has a meeting with the new king of India in a few weeks.

29

Miss Laila, Armed and Dangerous

EVERYTHING IS AS before, almost. Mukundan is in the WagonR, driving alone. Somewhere ahead on the highway is the little blue Indica with the couple inside, racing towards doom. But he is not tailing them any more. The Gypsy has taken over.

Outside the petrol station, as things turned out, he was a few seconds too late. He was about ten metres away from Jamal's car when he heard the sounds of the Sumo's doors open and shut. He could almost feel the Bureau men behind him. In a matter of seconds they would have taken control of the Indica and driven away. But there was a screech of tyres. The Gypsy veered off the highway and stopped beside them. Six cops in plain clothes emerged. They were from the Beard Squad. They had got wind of the operation. They asked Mukundan and the other Bureau officers to back off and get into their cars, but the Bureau stood its ground. There was a bit of shoving of chests among the men but Mukundan stayed out of the scuffle.

Jamal peeped out of the car window. He might have sensed that at least some of the men in the quarrel were cops because cops often look like cops. In fact, some cops look like cops only when they are in civilian clothes. But how was Jamal to guess that the fight concerned him, and that what he was witnessing was a stand-off between the Subsidiary Intelligence Bureau and the Beard Squad over when he must be abducted.

The men then decided to keep it low. They argued, almost in mutters but not whispers. Cops find whispering too deferential.

The leader of the Gypsy dispatch was a man with very powerful shoulders and whose head was shaven, surely for religious reasons, like penance after a murder. He said, calmly, 'We need the girl, too. And we need them to be together when we take them.'

'Why?' the Sumo's leader asked.

'Gods want it that way.'

'My boss wants the girl to be left out.'

'The Gujarat police wants the girl, and that's all that matters considering where you are standing. Just get into your cars. That's all you need to know.'

'Why do you need the girl?' Mukundan asked, with no hostility.

'Look, it's coming from very, very high up. Actually, this is beyond the police and the Bureau. Just get the hint, and leave. We need the girl. And what do you think she is, anyway? Mother Teresa? She is in with them.'

Mukundan weighed his options. He could walk up to the Indica and point a gun at Jamal. That would have forced everyone to go with the flow. But one of the Beards called Boss and that left Mukundan with no choice but to follow orders.

Boss called his phone and let out a string of expletives. It was not clear though if Boss was abusing him or the Beards.

'Sir, I don't know how they got to know.'

'You were too late,' Boss said.

'Sir, the situation is that the target is ten metres away. The girl is in the toilet. Ten seconds and we can still be off with the man. The girl will never know. We can fend off these cops if you ask us to.'

'Those bastards will get the girl anyway. They really want the girl. Just get back. Do as they say. Get back.'

The eleven men stood around, not sure of their next move. Someone began to smoke. Minutes passed. The girl emerged from the petrol station, looking for Jamal. He yelled from the car, 'Here,' and waved. In-between Jamal and the girl was a mob of men, their imminent abductors. The girl walked through them, her head bent. She was carrying bananas and water. In seconds, the Indica was gone. This girl, what an unlucky creature she is.

HE CAN SEE the high tin roof of the tollbooth. There are four booths, two on either side of the road. In one of the queues, the Gypsy is almost brushing the bumper of Jamal's Indica. Behind the Gypsy is the Sumo, followed by Mukundan's car. It is a long line to the tollbooth but it is a brisk line. As the vehicles ahead pay and leave, Jamal inches closer and closer towards the final moments of his freedom. Through the windscreens of the two cars ahead of him, Mukundan can see the contours of the couple. They are quiet. How much can two people talk.

But they must, they must say everything they wish to say to each other, and they must say it all in the next few seconds.

WHEN THE INDICA finally reaches the booth, Jamal's hand stretches out with cash but no one takes it. Three men in civilian clothes emerge from the booth, enter the vehicle through the rear doors and settle in the back seat. They may have shown a gun or just said 'drive' or whatever it is that cops say in such situations. The car moves. The Gypsy keeps a tight distance, securing the rear. An unmarked Qualis, idling a few metres ahead of the tollbooth, comes alive and leads the hijacked car into the shoulder of the highway and into a narrow deserted dark lane. Here, Jamal and the girl are transferred to the Qualis.

The girl, as she is held by the neck and arm, looks terrified. She screams. She looks at Jamal for clarity. He is quiet. It appears that he has an idea who the men are, and what is going on. In a minute, the Qualis is back on the highway. Mukundan's assignment is over, but he follows the abduction.

THE TOLLBOOTH WAS chosen as the site of abduction because the abductors needed the car to be stationary when they took control of it. But the chief reason, Mukundan had thought, was that the tollbooth was very close to the safe house. However, the Qualis has kept going. It travels about ninety minutes, covering nearly one hundred kilometres to the very rim of Ahmedabad. It enters an area of vast yawning darkness and finally stops at the massive iron gates of a farmhouse.

The farmhouse is probably set on a large orchard, he can see only a vacant night within. There is no sign of life inside until two men emerge from the darkness and open the gates. The vehicles drive in, past the two grave muscular men. Mukundan's car is the last to enter. The gates groan and shut behind him.

The Qualis stops on the porch, where there is space for only one vehicle to stand. The other vehicles stop a few metres away, on the driveway. There is a flurry of car doors opening and closing. When the doors of the Qualis open, there is not a sound from the girl. He had expected screams but she is probably done screaming. She walks, without being held. When the abductors are cops, their quarry usually imagine that they are still in the protection of the land. So they walk. Jamal, too, walks flanked by two wary men.

Three cops begin to inspect the Indica. As Mukundan makes his way towards the house, he catches a glimpse of the car's boot – there is nothing there.

THE LIVING ROOM of the farmhouse is dimly lit. The place is possibly owned by one of the Beard Squad cops. Not directly, of course. There is usually a rags-to-riches hotelier who is the front.

There are sixteen cops in the room, including Mukundan. Some are from the Bureau but most are from the lower rungs of the Beard Squad, at the level of sub-inspectors. The size of the team reassures him. When the Beard Squad carries out executions, it keeps its team very small. Most of the time, it is just Bhim and three other Beards, including his personal bodyguard. Such a team, according to their official version, would have tried to confront the terrorists, who would have opened fire and the Squad would have retaliated, leaving all the terrorists dead.

The fact that Bhim allowed such a large team to be a part of the abduction probably suggests that he does not plan to execute Jamal and the girl. It is unlikely that he will change his mind later. Eyewitnesses can be very expensive. But it is not clear to Mukundan what the Beard Squad plans to do with the couple. If they were to be released into formal custody, the Squad and the Bureau would have to explain the abduction of the girl. Of Jamal, too, but nobody cares so much about the abduction of a male terror suspect. Mukundan is missing something.

Considering the failed mutiny a few hours ago, nobody is paying particular attention to him. The bald stud, who had put his stone hand on Mukundan's chest outside the petrol station, is standing near the fridge, fiddling with his phone. Some of the cops are in a huddle on sofas, talking in faint voices. Some are eating alone from steel boxes their wives may have packed. The couple is not here; they have been lodged in two adjacent bedrooms on the ground floor. He gathers that the girl is alone in her room, for the moment. Jamal, in his cell, is being interrogated by Boss and Bhim.

There is no one else in Jamal's room. Obviously, they don't think he is lethal. And it appears the interrogation is really just that. There are no wails of a man pleading with other men to stop brutalizing him. In any case, Boss and Red Beard are not the ones who do the beating. They have thin wrists. Beating up even a captive man is a lot of hard work.

After about an hour, the two cops emerge from Jamal's room, chatting. They do not look like men who had a stormy fight a few hours ago. They must have made their peace. They look more like accomplices now. They are laughing over something. Mukundan has never seen Bhim in flesh before. His face is magnified by his red mane, and he has narrow shrewd eyes. There is something of the feline in him. It's probably his small mouth and nose and the efficient body. Boss is a few inches taller than Bhim. He is dark, balding and greying; the sort of man whose lips gather saliva at the edges.

Bhim and Boss, still chatting, stop outside the girl's room. A sub-inspector, who has a ring of keys as though he is the mother-in-law of the house, unlocks the door and leaves. Bhim throws a casual glance across the living room and his narrow eyes fall on Mukundan. Boss says something to Bhim and the man laughs. Boss gives Mukundan a nod as the two men enter the girl's room, chatting. The door shuts.

Mukundan tries to lurk near the door but he is unable to hear anything, not even the questions of the men. After about thirty minutes, the interrogators emerge. They do not look very disturbed or pleased.

Boss takes an apple from the fridge and approaches Mukundan. 'You did well,' he says with a kind smile, studying the fruit. 'You can go now.'

'Can I spend the night here?' he asks. 'And leave early?'

Boss does not like the request. 'No, no, no,' he says. 'You can rest for a while. But leave, leave tonight.'

'Sir.'

'Leave in an hour. Max. An hour.'

Mukundan joins the other men in the living room, where Bhim is signing papers. Two inspectors had been waiting to get the signatures from him on paperwork concerning security arrangements in the city. He looks up from the papers to take a good look at Mukundan. He chuckles as he signs. When the paperwork is done, he comes to him and puts his arm around his shoulder, and they walk around the room. Everybody else is watching.

'You're angry with us?' Bhim says.

'No, sir. Why would I be?'

'I heard you raised your voice with our men.'

'I didn't raise my voice, sir. You're confusing me for someone else.'

'Your Boss was very angry with us. But I've managed to convince him.'

'That's good, sir.'

'I'm not a bad man. I'm a poet. Do you know that I'm a poet?'

'I didn't know, sir.'

'Can I tell you what kind of a man I am?'

'Yes, sir.'

'If I was a football star, imagine I am a football star with a top European club; when I score a goal, and my teammates come running to me, I am not the type of man who would push them away or try to evade them just to run to the cameras and flail my hands. I would instead hug my teammates and shake their hands.'

'That's good, sir.'

'I take my men along.'

'Got it, sir.'

'Why did we get the girl? Is that what my boy is thinking? Why did we take the girl?'

'We did what we had to, sir. It's over.'

'Your Hindi is hilarious. You from the south?'

'Yes, sir.'

'Last week I watched a film on TV. It's called *King Kong*. Have you heard of *King Kong*?'

'Yes, sir.'

'Have you seen the film?'

'No, sir.'

'In *King Kong*, some white people go to a remote island, which is filled with giant magical creatures the world has never seen. I think they are hunters. Those white people, I think, they hunt exotic animals. So they are in this island filled with amazing animals, giant beasts. There are dinosaurs, and massive birds. But do you know what they capture and take to New York? An ape. They take back only the giant ape, not the other exotic beasts. Isn't that funny?'

'Now that you put it this way, sir, it is very strange.'

'And what's the name of the giant ape, my friend?'

'King Kong.'

'Exactly. You know what I was thinking. Why did those men take the ape and leave the dinosaurs behind?'

'I don't know, sir.'

'Because the film is called *King Kong*. That's why.'

The man lets out a slow laugh. 'What morons,' he says.

He knocks his forehead on Mukundan gently. He smells of shampoo, which is rare for a cop.

'True that our operation had Jamal's name on it, son, but if we find an exotic creature in his car, only a moron would leave her behind. So we took her in and asked some polite questions. We are going to ask more questions. You just watch. She is going to sing. A simple innocent college girl does not set out on an adventure with a married man. She is with them, she knows them, she is one of them.'

'Has she confessed, sir?'

Bhim moves back a few inches to show a dramatic interest in him.

'First two hours, they are all very strong.'

'And what about Jamal, sir?'

Bhim looks around, studying all the eyes that are on him, and he laughs. He pokes his finger on Mukundan's chest.

'What a cop,' Bhim says. 'This boy is a cop. Forget what he said, Mukundan, let me tell you what I told him.'

'Tell me, sir.'

'I told him a joke.'

'What's the joke, sir?'

'A fidayeen who had blown himself for Allah goes to heaven. He searches for seventy-two virgins but finds only seventy-two horny young black boys waiting for him. The fidayeen screams at God. Where are my seventy-two virgins you promised?'

Bhim says 'virgins' in English, which is probably essential for the joke to work.

'And God said, "Look, I said seventy-two virgins, I never said "girls".'

The room erupts in laughter. Bhim, even as he laughs, puts his hand in Mukundan's pocket and fishes out his mobile phone.

'Sony. You have a Sony. Not bad for an honest cop.'

'My sister gifted it, sir.'

'Does your phone take photographs?'

'Yes, sir.'

Bhim goes through the photographs.

'You didn't take any pictures of them, son.'

'Who, sir?'

'Our guests. Our couple.'

'No, sir.'

'Why not?'

'I was not asked to, sir.'

'Good,' he says. 'Good.'

'Thanks, sir.'

Boss, finally, speaks. 'He's a fine boy.'

'Your boss thinks she is innocent,' Bhim tells Mukundan. 'What do you feel?'

'I don't know, sir.'

'Are you wondering what we would do if she is innocent?'

'What will you do, sir?'

'Don't you know?'

'No, sir?'

'That we let people go?'

A ringtone begins and that brings about a calm. It is Bhim's phone. He turns reverential, but not subservient. He walks to a corner. It is hard to hear him clearly but there is no doubt he is speaking to someone very important.

In a few minutes, Boss leaves the farmhouse with another fresh apple. Bhim and two other senior officers, too, leave. The rest stay in the living room.

Mukundan mingles but he gathers very little. The rooms where Jamal and the girl are detained are barren, he is told. The windows are sealed, even the fans removed. They are handcuffed and have been instructed to sit on the floor, in a corner, at all times. They are free to urinate in their clothes.

And, the girl's name is Laila Raza. She is nineteen.

Mukundan thinks of a way to extend his stay in the farmhouse. He lies on a fat rug. There are other men who are sleeping, on couches, chairs and the floor. Maybe he can just lurk around, and if no one remembers to kick him out he can claim that he had dozed off.

He must have been very tired, he really does doze off. He is woken up by the familiar sounds of a man wailing. The man's sounds are faint and when he speaks he says that he is a father of three kids. That's all he says. A preliminary beating is under way in Jamal's room. The men probably have no questions for him. The questions will come later, after Jamal feels worthless. It is surprising how swiftly a man can be made to feel he is nothing. When a man feels he is nothing, he loses his ideology and convictions. Then he is filled only with facts. Mukundan keeps an eye on the girl's door. As far as he can tell, there is no one in the room but her. She is probably crouched in a corner, trying to shut out the sounds of the man.

A Bureau cop, one of the men who had tailed Jamal in the Sumo, walks up to Mukundan, his phone to the ear. 'What are you still doing here?' the man says.

'I dozed off.'

'Boss is asking you to get out.'

Mukundan leaves. He feels as though he has left a child at the mercy of over a dozen men. What must he do, what must an insignificant young man do?

He drives out of the farmhouse, and in a minute merges with the highway traffic.

If morality is, as he believes, a system of logic where a moral choice is wise because it is the only path that conscience shows while the other paths, the ambiguous ways, are many, the right course of action for him is to extract the girl from the farmhouse and put her in formal judicial custody.

He has a fair idea how to do it. He has to let some friends know about the farmhouse, who would in turn let the TV channels and human rights activists know. If he is careful, he might even get away with it. But then that would force the Beard Squad to implicate her as a terrorist. They would have no choice. That would be the only way they can save a bit of their skin. She may spend decades in prison.

He tries to understand, not for the first time, why Bhim has taken the abduction of a teenage girl so lightly. The Squad might be protected by very powerful men but these days there are limits to the powers of powerful men. If news channels get to know that a nineteen-year-old girl was held in illegal custody by about twenty policemen, it would be disastrous for all the officers involved. Even if the bosses deny everything she claims, a fact has a mysterious endurance, and there would be too much attention from journalists, a lot of whom are women these days, and human rights activists, who are mostly women, and Muslim politicians. Some careers would end. And, it is too late for Bhim to solve the problem by shooting Jamal and the girl in their heads and claiming there was a gun battle. There are too many people involved in the abduction of the couple.

What if she is, in fact, deeply involved in terror? He knows nothing about her at all. And what if she is actually in no physical danger at all? Maybe Bhim really does plan to let her go, persuade her to keep her mouth shut, and to even use her as an informer. It happens all the time.

So, the situation is that if Mukundan tries to save her, he might end up putting her in prison. If he leaves her alone, she might get back to her life tomorrow morning.

But the spectre of the shut door does not leave him. A girl in absolute dread behind a shut door. He pulls over. What must a man do?

30

A Patriarch's Review

THE FIRST MOMENTS inside the aircraft are, as usual, ominous. The young air hostess, who is stunning, frames life as too precious. In the open cockpit, one of the two pilots is too serious, too quiet. The bearded technician standing with them, holding a pad, seems to know a secret. He is surely a devout Muslim.

In the business section, where Professor Vaid is seated, there is only him. He is always embarrassed by the luxury, but only during boarding when people shuffle in throwing unpleasant glances at the business class. Nobody recognizes him any more, which is good. But the crew knows who he is. That is because the patriots have informed them. Someone from the airline had escorted him to the gate. The army boy had apologized for frisking him.

As the plane taxis towards the queue to the runway, his phone rings. That draws the attention of the lone stewardess in the business section. He wishes to switch off the device but it is AK on the line.

'I am in the plane.'

'Are you sitting?'

'Yes. Why do you ask?'

'This is going to make you laugh very hard, Professor.'

The flight attendant walks to the patriarch's seat and stands looking unhappy and reverential at once.

'Our friend in the debris, Professor. He says Jamal and the girl are on their way to Ahmedabad.'

'I see.'

'They are not carrying a bomb, they are going to meet some friends.'

'Why is that funny?'

'Jamal and the girl are going to Ahmedabad, Professor.'

'Why are you laughing, AK?'

'Sir,' the flight attendant says, 'I'm very sorry, you have to switch off your phone. We're about to take off.'

'They are in a little blue car, Professor.'

'A little blue car?'

'It is an Indica. They're going to meet a sleeper cell that is planning to assassinate Damodarbhai. A blue Indica. Mumbra to Ahmedabad. The man's name is Jamal. Jamal.'

'You don't think this is ...'

'Exactly. And the girl's name, Professor, is Laila Raza.'

'Oh no.'

'Sir,' the flight attendant says. She is not stern yet, but almost there. 'I'm sorry, sir, you have to switch off your phone.'

'AK, I have to go.'

'The entire intel and police system has been going crazy all day. For this. For our Jamal and Laila.'

'Who's the man in the debris, then?'

'We'll soon know.'

'He has to be a cop, AK.'

'I agree.'

THE ENGINES SCREAM, the plane gathers speed on the runway and it begins to sound like a disaster. As the plane leaves ground, he sees fireworks over Mumbai. The patriots have begun their celebration.

The economy class is full. In its front row, six feet diagonally behind Vaid is a wailing baby in the arms of an unhappy mother. The infant has been this way even before take-off. The curtain separating the business cabin and the economy is still parted. The mother can see him, and the empty business section, too. He is not looking at her with even a hint of annoyance but she returns his gaze with a glare as though he is responsible for her circumstances. She is flanked by two middle-aged men, who do not appear to be related to her. They throw glances at the baby, which is unusually loud and miserable. The infant, a girl, and the mother have drawn the attention of other passengers too. Is she going to travel like this, holding a wailing newborn in her arms?

That is what the other passengers, especially in the front rows of the economy class, are surely thinking. Some murmurs grow. There is talk about how empty the business section is. Vaid has a fair idea what is about to occur. The passengers will play their hand wrong. They will do it the activist way.

The seat-belt sign goes off, the crew gets busy with the food trays. The infant has not stopped wailing. The curtain separating the classes is drawn but through the gaps Vaid follows the beginnings of a revolt.

One of the men flanking the mother, the balding man on the aisle seat, makes the predictable request to a stewardess. He asks her to transfer the mother and the infant to the business class. It is not a bad move but the man is unable to avoid the moralizing tone. 'This should have been obvious to the crew,' he says. The hostess says she would consider the request but she does nothing. Soon, as the cries of the baby escalate, the man makes a more forceful request. He is joined by a few other passengers, including the mother, of course.

They admonish the crew, thereby claiming a high moral position. But there was a reason why the crew had not upgraded the woman in the first place. There is a reason why things are the way they are and the reason is often very good.

Insulted by a moral reprimand, the airline crew now resists by showing a higher moral cause – they claim that there is regulation against late upgrades, and that there are other women with infants in the economy class who may demand to become refugees in the business class when their infants begin to cry. The crew does not mention a more practical reason, which is that the old man in the business section is a patriarch of the Sangh and he may not like it if his island of peace is treated as a daycare.

When activism is surprised by excellent reasons against its moral cause, it feels compelled to defame the reasons. So the passengers begin to accuse the crew of inventing spurious reasons. The activists thus shift from a moral cause to a wrong premise. Everything that they would do from this point will be a waste of time. Some middle-aged men may receive general appreciation for exhibiting their low-stakes goodness, but the mother will continue to travel in great misery. The story of the nation.

There is a simpler way to upgrade the woman.

He wonders what Miss Iyer would think of the moral passengers of the flight. Would she view their protest as activism or as an act of decency? She would probably see activism. The passengers who demand that the mother be upgraded have self-interest, a latent contempt for the unattainable business class, and so badly want to shame the system that casts them as lesser citizens that they exploit the misery of a circumstantial underclass – the mother with an infant-in-arms. The primary intent of the moralizing passengers is not the welfare of the mother.

A patriarch and a modern young woman are natural foes, yet Miss Iyer and he see something in the goodness syndicate that most people cannot. They can see a feudal system where the strong use the weak to attack the stronger.

In the film *Longest Hunger Strike on Earth*, Miss Iyer goes to meet Sharmila, a woman who has refused to have food or water for the past fifteen years in protest against a law that gives the Indian armed forces extraordinary powers to violate human rights. She has also refused to comb her hair or look at herself in a mirror. The government has not intervened in these sacrifices. She is almost a free woman. The only thing the government ensures is that it feeds her through a tube that passes through her nose and reaches her stomach.

The film opens with Sharmila studying her fingers as though waiting for the interview to begin. Her face is in a perpetual grimace. A tube emerges from beneath her shawl and runs into her nose. There is the sound of a door opening. Sharmila looks up, and she looks shocked. Then an uncertain smile comes to her face.

When Miss Iyer enters the frame, it is evident why Sharmila was so surprised. Miss Iyer has inserted a tube into her own nose. 'This is horrible,' she says.

'Are you making fun of me?'

'It's horrible, Sharmila, to live with a tube up your nose.'

'There are worse things in this world.'

'Why is the government trying to feed you when you keep telling the courts you don't wish to die?'

'They don't believe me.'

'They must know that if you really wanted to die, you would have died by now. You're not that type. You wish to live.'

'I love life. That's all I tell the Indian government. I love life.'

'Why are you going through this?' Miss Iyer says, tugging gently at Sharmila's nasal tube.

'For my people,' Sharmila says.

'That's what the activists around you have trained you to say. They have employed you, Sharmila, as a saint with a tube up her nose. Sainthood is a form of employment, you know that, right?'

'Are you really a journalist?'

'You're in love. There is a man who loves you, Sharmila. You keep all his letters in a box and you read them. You want to live like a person, not a saint.'

'I think you must leave.'

'Are you stuck with this "iron lady" act? Are you stuck, Sharmila? There is no shame in giving up. You know that. There is no shame.'

There is the sound of a door opening and the exclamation of a man. In a moment, a dozen people rush in and they evict Miss Iyer and the cameraperson, who is unseen. 'Don't touch my tube, guys,' Miss Iyer says on her way out. 'It's my breakfast.'

THE INFANT IS more furious than ever. The patriarch can see through the slit of the curtain that the mother is on the verge of tears. She should consider crying. The modern age of compassion requires the victim to first surrender pride, only then can justice be done. But what may help her more in this situation is the arrival of an obnoxious man.

The obnoxious man, in reality, should be a caricature of an obnoxious man. His objective is to transfer the woman and the infant to comfort. To that end it is important that he appears despicable. He would scream at the all-female crew, he would tell them that the mother and the infant are a nuisance, and he would demand that he be transferred to the vacant business class. He would set in motion the first principles of a fable. He would gift the all-female crew a familiar oppressor – a man who reminds them of other oppressors from their private lives. He would hand them an opportunity to vanquish a villain. As a result, out of self-interest, they would perform a moral act. To spite him they would upgrade the miserable mother instead of him. The passengers would cheer. The true hero would be disgraced, but he would have achieved his end. Bureaucrats and cops do exactly this every day in the great republic. The most effective activists are people who are never known as activists, just as the deadliest anarchists are never known as anarchists.

The patriarch rises and walks into the economy class. From the far end of the plane, a stewardess comes marching towards him with a confused smile. He goes up to the mother in the front row and takes the infant from her. Before she fully realizes what is going on, the infant is in his arms. The baby is stunned into silence and is perhaps further persuaded to shut up by the vapours of aromatic oils on his old body. He carries away the infant to the business class. The mother follows. The cabin erupts.

Can you hear this, Akhila, the applause of fools?

31

Around 8 p.m.

THIS TIME, CRAWLING into the tunnel feels like a journey into the womb of a giant selfish mother. There is even a helpless life lodged inside, if Akhila may milk the poor metaphor dry. This has occurred to her only now because sentimental poetry never comes easily to her, as though it fears her rational insults.

Her arms ache and her powerful core is collapsing, but she wants to do this as long as she can. She wants to crawl on her belly to the man, check his pulse, feed him saline and tell him that he is going to be alright. There is meaning in this. Before this day, she has never been crucial to anyone. Ma taught her, though she didn't mean to, that exceptional altruism is a kind of madness, and Akhila has for long been suspicious of its lure. Even in her decision to study medicine, she had assured herself, the idea of saving lives was peripheral. She only wished to be consumed by science and to be far away from liberal arts, far from all the long spectral tentacles of Ma.

She can't wait to get to the man. It has been over half an hour since she last examined him. Any moment he may slip into shock. Where the tunnel turns steep, she begins to crawl faster.

But is this really about meaning, or is it just a family tic? Is she, too, like Ma, addicted to rescues?

When she reaches him, she goes through a set of actions that have become routine, and she does them without looking at his face. The lifeless leg of the woman who is embedded in the rubble, her silver anklet glowing in Akhila's headlamp, has now acquired the quality of a familiar ad on a hoarding.

There is the dull drone of a drill. It is the sound of a soldier digging the other tunnel to pull the man out head first. She checks the pulse in his foot. He is beginning to do well. It is as though he is responding to a fundamental change in the way everybody above the ground has begun to perceive him. The past several hours, she had attended to him with caution. He was after all a terror suspect. She could not despise him or even be deeply afraid of him, he was so helpless, but still, he was a man who knew too much about a terror operation. But the last time she examined him, he uttered one word that changed everything. He said many other things, but most important, he said, 'Laila.'

Jamal and Laila. Now everybody knows what he has been talking about. Jamal and Laila from Mumbra in a little car on their way to Ahmedabad. Everyone knows that story. The mention of Jamal alone had meant nothing. But that name when taken with Laila made everything fall in place. The new theory among the police officers is that this man is a cop.

*

SHE STABS HIS marrow with saline. This time he reacts. His leg shudders in acute pain. She checks his face and there is no doubt that his eyes see her. He has been staring.

'Do you see me,' she says in Hindi, which she had long settled on as their official language even though he did mumble on occasion in Malayalam.

'Do you see me?'

She crawls across the beam and slithers over him as she has done many times. Her face is just inches over him but he has shut his eyes. 'Open your eyes,' she says. He says something. His voice is not as faint as before but the sound of the drills drowns it. She puts her ear to his mouth.

'Your light is hurting my eyes,' he says.

She laughs. 'I didn't think of that.' She turns off her headlamp. He studies her closely in the faint glow of the torchlights she has left around him. In his eyes there is now life and presence. He is probably wondering how a girl like her ended up on top of a man like him in a place like this.

It was easier to lie on top of him when he was delirious. Now that he is alert, she feels awkward. Also, with the arrival of sense in his eyes, he appears younger than she had thought. Under forty, surely.

'You can see me, you can hear me?' she says.

'Yes.'

'You said, "yes"?'

'Yes.'

Akhila feels a surge of joy hearing him respond to her for the very first time. She wants to put her head on his chest and laugh. The drill in the alternative tunnel falls silent, as though the soldier who is digging it wants to eavesdrop. 'What's your name?' she asks.

'How long have I been here?'

'I think it is a good idea if I don't tell you.'

'How long?'

'What's your name?'

'Mukundan.'

'Murugan?'

'No. Mukundan.'

'Are you a Malayalee or a Tamilian?'

'Malayalee.'

'I can speak a bit of Malayalam but Malayalees say I shouldn't.'

He smiles, actually smiles.

'In the morning, you were in a building. It fell. You're buried in the debris.'

'I figured.'

'Do you live here? I mean did you live here?'

'How long have I been here?'

'What matters is that we are very close to getting you out.'

'Are you speaking the truth?'

'I swear.'

'Please remove me somehow.'

'Am I heavy?'

'I don't understand your question.'

'Am I heavy on your chest?'

'I don't know.'

'Can you breathe easily?'

'I think so.'

'Your speech is smooth.'

'Am I going to make it?'

'Yes, I promise. Do you feel any injury in your back or neck?'

'I don't know.'

'I've given you a lot of painkillers.'

'Are you a doctor?'

'Yes.'

'I can't move my legs.'

'There is a huge beam over them, but not entirely on them. Your blood flow is fine but you won't be able to move your legs.'

'Chop off my legs. Get me out.'

'We may not have to do that now. The soldiers tried to chop off this beam but it was taking too long. So they have started digging another tunnel. You heard the drill? Mukundan, do you hear the drill behind you.'

'Yes.'

'That is the other tunnel coming to you.'

'Will they chop off my legs?'

'No. They plan to use a carjack to lift the beam that is over your legs, and they will pull you out.'

'How long will that take?'

'Mukundan, are you a cop?'

'Yes. I am with the Bureau.'

'Does that mean the Intelligence Bureau?'

'Yes.'

'You were saying something about Jamal and Laila.'

He begins to pant. She lifts her body to give him relief. When he recovers, she bends closer to him.

'What did I say?'

'You were saying that they were in a blue Indica and they were going somewhere. You were saying that the cops planned to abduct them and kill them.'

'I said that?'

'Yes'

'That happened a long time ago,' Mukundan says.

'Yes. Eight years ago. Nine?'

'Ten years ago.'

'Ten years ago. Yes. That's right.'

'That happened ten years ago.'

'Why were you mumbling about something that happened ten years ago?'

'I don't know.'

'All day the cops thought you were talking about something that is under way.'

'There are cops outside?'

'Yes.'

'How long before you get me out?'

'Don't shut your eyes. Mukundan, you have to keep your eyes open. Did you live here? Do you have children? Mukundan, wake up.'

HE CAN HEAR her but a powerful sleep comes over him. He has been very confused in the time that preceded the conversation. What he remembers is waking up several times and finding himself entombed and unable to move, as though he has fallen hard on his back. He remembers praying for sleep.

Early in the morning, he had walked to the one-room home of a childhood friend, whose name he has forgotten. The plan was to have breakfast with him and watch election news. The friend's young wife opened the door. He remembers her name. Bindu was probably annoyed that she had to wear a sari so early in the day. She managed a smile but as usual never met his eyes. She walked away in the sounds of silver anklets. Her feet were turmeric yellow, he remembers that. And he remembers telling himself that it is alright to watch the soft feet of a loyal friend's young wife.

He removed his shoes in the doorway and walked into a tiny kitchen where there was the smell of strong filter coffee. It is odd, the things a man remembers about a morning he has mostly forgotten. The friend was having his bath in a corner of the kitchen, behind a plastic curtain. 'Go inside. I am done in a minute,' he yelled. Mukundan took out his phone and the bulky wallet and left them on the kitchen platform. He walked into the living room, the only room, and sat on the floor.

The moment he sat, he felt giddy. It was unusual, he never feels giddy. 'Here,' the lady said, holding a glass of water. He must have looked so blank she laughed. But her face soon turned grave. The glass fell from her hand, the room began to tremble. A clock fell; an idol, too. Vessels in the kitchen rolled down. Humans, finally, made their sounds in all the homes. Then a stillness arrived but it was brief.

There was a morbid yawn from somewhere deep in the earth. The room heaved and sank, Bindu fell on him, screaming. He saw the roof cave in and a family plunge towards him with all their things.

When he woke up, there was perfect darkness and a deep silence. He had never been more certain that he was alive. There was so much pain in him but he was not sure where exactly. He has never experienced pain without knowing where he was hurt. He was probably so damaged, and in so many places, his brain was confused. He knew he was buried but he had forgotten how. There was something immense and immovable on him. He passed out.

What he then saw in his mind was not as unreliable as a dream. It had happened, all of it. He was only seeing his memory, but he had no control over how it flowed. He could not stop the visions. He saw himself the way he was ten years ago.

He was waiting for a man on a street. He had been waiting since dawn. He had arrived before the muezzin's first lament of the day. Had watched the morning come and the street fill with scrawny and stunted young Muslim men in small jeans, old men with orange beards, a few women here and there in hijab, little children walking carefully to school in the gaps between open sewers and puddles. Any time now, Jamal would appear and get into a blue Indica.

When Mukundan emerged from the vision, he was once again in his tomb. He kept slipping in and out of deep sleep in this manner. Once, when he opened his eyes the tomb was not dark any more. There was a faint light around him. Someone had left electric lamps for him. Then a new light arrived, brighter, shifting, alive. He heard a girl say something in Hindi. She sounded posh. Moments later, he felt a sharp pain as though someone had stabbed him with a pen but he didn't know where. And he felt a heaviness crawl over him. The light grew.

NOW HE UNDERSTANDS that the approaching and fading light was always this girl who is lying on top of him.

He wants to know what exactly he has been mumbling. From what the girl has told him, it is clear that he has been rambling about that day when he had shadowed Jamal and Laila, the day he recalls every moment of his life.

That is bad, very bad, but he might be able to contain the damage. After all, he was dying. He is not a traitor, he was just a dying man who was not in his senses. He hopes he has not said much about what followed the night Laila was captured.

AS IT TURNED out, at the end of that long night, Mukundan did not rescue Laila from the farmhouse. Instead, he drove for seven hours to the heart of Mumbai, deposited the car in Bureau's care and took a bus home.

Two days later, early morning, he saw the news on TV. He threw up where he sat. That was all he did that morning. But he did not feel anger or guilt or even sorrow. He only felt queasy. When that was done, he set out to find out what had happened.

THREE WEEKS BEFORE he was asked to shadow Jamal, the Beard Squad had abducted two Pakistani terrorists, Rambo-1 and Rambo-2. They were taken minutes after they reached

Ahmedabad by train. They were held in two safe houses and put on wiretap. Among those who called Rambo-1 was Jamal Sheikh. Jamal had been employed by a man in Dubai to run supplies for the Rambos. The first delivery was four illegal satphones. Rambo-1, following the instructions of the Bureau and the Beard Squad, asked Jamal to go to Ahmedabad with the phones. The cops set a trap. They were hoping that he would pick up other suspects, but he picked up a girl. The Bureau did not want to abduct the girl, but the Beards of the crime branch wanted her.

On the first night of captivity, Jamal confessed to his association with Rambo-1. About Laila Raza, he said she was under the impression that they were going to meet garment merchants. But the girl did not speak a word. After she was abducted, and her screams died in the vehicle, she and Jamal exchanged a glance. She did not utter a word after that. She said nothing during the two days and three nights she was imprisoned in the farmhouse. But the cops did not touch her. They only repeated their questions and left.

On the third night of their abduction, Rambo-1 was taken to the farmhouse. He, Jamal and Laila were blindfolded and driven to a section of a desolate road. There, an unmarked vehicle brought Rambo-2, who too was blindfolded. The blue Indica was parked in the middle of the road. Half a kilometre away, two cops diverted the thin approaching traffic.

Laila, Jamal, and the Rambos were made to stand near the Indica. They stood in their blindfolds, but their hands were free.

Eight Beards, including Bhim, opened fire. Some rounds were fired on the blue car. The Beards also fired at bushes and the road from a different set of weapons – six AK-56 rifles, which they left near the four bodies. The guns were a gift from the Bureau, from its stash of confiscated weapons. But the Beards forgot to get the fingerprints of the dead on the guns. They would realize that only days later. But it didn't matter.

After the four were killed, their bodies were laid out on the wayside. At sunrise the press landed. The official story was that the police had got a tip-off about four Lashkar-e-Taiba terrorists who were travelling in a blue Indica. They tried to stop the car, the terrorists opened fire. As usual, no cop was injured but all the terrorists died. The police identified the three men by their names. Laila was, at first, called 'unknown young woman', but as the day progressed the police released her name. They said she was a suicide bomber. She was not strapped to a bomb, though. 'Like a writer is not strapped to pen,' Bhim told the journalists, 'and a photographer is not always strapped to a camera. But have no doubts, at the time of her death, Miss Laila was armed and dangerous.'

She lay on the road, her arms and legs spread, one shoe missing, mouth open, eyes open.

IN THE MORGUE, four low-caste men sat like giant frogs on the corpses and removed the innards. It was not a task for higher people. Outside, an old rubber farmer from Kerala arrived to see the body of his son.

Parents waiting to collect the bodies of their children – Mukundan has watched the sight many times. Usually they stood, sometimes with hands on the hips; sometimes leaning on the wall; or with a hand on a human, any human. They sat, too. They didn't always cry. They ate, they even spoke on the phone.

Jamal's father was alone. He was an elegant man with orderly silver hair and the sharp nose of a high-caste Malayalee. The widower looked like the kind of man who would have many friends and two generations of relatives, but they might have thought it unwise to accompany him.

'My father looks a lot like you,' Mukundan lied in Malayalam.

Even in those circumstances, the old man lit up when he heard his language. He was far from home.

'My son looks a lot like you.' He lied, too. But then he said, 'I am sorry I said that.'

'Why must you be sorry. I am sure I look a lot like your son.'

'You won't say that if you know about my son. Do you know what they say about my son?'

'I know your son. Everybody here knows your son.'

'I am waiting for my son.'

'I know.'

'When they give him to me, I will take him in a box, in a plane. Imagine taking your child in a box. Should I just take him in a car? It's cheaper. I am told you can't take your son in a box in a train. That's not allowed.'

'Is there anything I can do to help you?'

'I am a Hindu.'

'I thought so.'

'My son was a Hindu.'

'What happened then?'

'He became a Muslim because he loved a woman. Do you hate him? Do you hate my son?'

'I don't hate your son.'

'There are men in this world who only wish to sleep with women and dump them. My son relinquished his religion for love. He became a Muslim. Of all the things, a Muslim. He was a lover. Some men are like that. They are lovers. They can't help it. He was not a terrorist. He didn't care about Allah. He only cared about his wife and his kids.'

'Have you eaten anything this morning?'

'There must have been so much dirt on the road.'

'I don't follow what you're saying.'

'On the road where they put his body for the world to see. It was so dirty. They put my son on the road.'

'Yes.'

'When my son was a boy and he used to fall down and get hurt, I could not bear to see his wound. Parents are retards. They cannot bear to see even a scratch on their child's knee. But you know what I saw on TV? My blood-soaked son lying on the road. Couldn't they have at least had the decency to cover his face? Didn't they think, the boy's father might be watching TV?'

'Can I get you some tea?'

'My country shot my son. The fence itself ate the crop.'

The old man's face became a slow rustic scowl. It was a scowl Mukundan used to see only on old Malayalee women. Do old men acquire some traits of old women?

'It's that girl,' he said. 'That Laila girl.'

'What about her?'

'It was her plan. She was the one who was on her way to meeting the terrorists. She knew my son dealt in satphones. She lured my son into this.'

THE CORPSES OF the Rambos were helpful in identifying their country of origin. They were carrying Pakistani passports on them, freshly printed passports. But the passports were entirely in English with not a word in Urdu. The Beards had never been under pressure to be competent. It was not surprising that they got even the Pakistani passport wrong. They didn't have to fabricate any such evidence but they did because that was their habit.

The bodies of the Rambos were not claimed by anyone. They were buried in secrecy in a government dump. Prayers were said, of course. Prayers, always. The republic has great respect for the dead.

WHEN LAILA'S BODY reached Mumbra, thousands of Muslims gathered around her coffin. They had no evidence but they knew that she had been murdered in cold blood. A lot of people, who were not Muslim, who were even important people, were saying the same thing on TV. Her body was carried through the streets of the filthy suburb where she was born and raised. Crowds chanted that she was not a terrorist.

Days later, her mother made a mistake. She told journalists that a few hours after Laila left home, she had called her, which was true because Mukundan had seen the girl in a phone booth, and he had, later, obtained the records of the phone she had used. She had called home. Her mother said that her daughter had sounded terrified because Jamal had brought 'two strange men along'.

Mother had fallen for the Beard Squad's tale about three men in the car and she had fabricated a little lie to disengage her daughter from those men. The Beard Squad now had Laila's mother on record claiming that the girl was, indeed, in a car with three men who had direct links to terror.

Mukundan did not seek to know if Laila Raza was indeed a terrorist. He did wonder why she had fallen silent after she had been abducted. It was not the act of silence that was intriguing but the capacity for silence. But he did not wish to know beyond the fact that the Beards themselves were not sure whether Laila Raza was a terrorist. It really did not matter, it would not alter what Mukundan had decided to do.

SINCE HER MURDER, Mukundan has often explained her death to Laila. During those moments, she is seated in front of a blue screen and stares at him without opinion as if he is about to take her passport-size photograph. It is this face of Laila that has endured in national memory. A pretty girl with a blank smile in a cheap provincial studio. Many believe she was a terrorist, many believe she was just in the wrong car, but almost no one believes she died in a gun battle.

It might outrage Laila but there is a fact he whispers to her now and then. Bhim decided to kill her because in his view it was simpler that way. Nothing personal.

The Squad always knew they would execute the Rambos and any small fry who fell into the net, like Jamal. No courts, no prison. The Beards knew what they had to do, they had done it many times before. Red Beard was actually thrilled when he got to know that a girl had fallen in the trap. People were getting bored of dead male terrorists on the highways. Television channels, too. Laila would return the Beards to fame. She did.

Laila might find some dignity in the knowledge that the Beard Squad was under severe attack from humanitarians. Some days it did look like the Beards had made a major miscalculation. Those days it seemed that the republic was not a sham. But then the Squad was in the care of Damodarbhai, and Damodarbhai was in the care of the times.

There was a state government inquiry. That was expected. But the objective of the inquiry was not to find out how Laila and the others died but to see who would rat on the Squad. Everyone who was involved in the operation got to know. That was the idea, perhaps. The message was that there would be many inquiries and none of them might be genuine. Everyone stuck to the official story. Four deadly terrorists, one of them a female suicide bomber. Mukundan was so insignificant, the investigators did not even summon him. And the last thing he wanted to do was approach them.

The Squad thrived. The Beards were rewarded with postings, houses and cash, so much cash that they had to hide it in metal boxes and bury them. Some did go to jail for a few days. But, eventually, everybody who killed Laila and Jamal got away.

TEN YEARS AFTER the murder of Laila Raza, Mukundan is still a bachelor, still a beacon for women in doomed relationships. A bachelor patriot, that is what he is. Like Damodarbhai.

THE GIRL IN the tunnel who is trying to save him fixes an oxygen mask on him. The mask is attached to a small inflated bag. What wonderful things are available in the nation these days to save a buried man. It is as though the republic believes a human life is precious.

A great rush of pure air fills his lungs. She must have done this many times. Slithered into the tunnel, checked on him, stabbed him with fluids and filled him with air.

He sees her crawl away like a giant lizard. Something about her makes him feel that he is going to live. The next time he is able to speak, he will ask her name. He hopes it is an easy Indian name. Or, at least, Nicole, which is easy too.

The way she is and the way she departs with wise calculations in her head remind him of another day when he had abandoned a girl stranded in a farmhouse filled with cops.

As her light leaves him, he feels a sudden terror. He wants to scream and beg her not to leave him.

AKHILA IS DESPERATE for fresh air but she reminds herself that she must not crawl too fast towards the mouth of the tunnel. If she had enough air in her lungs, she would have asked what she wished to ask before he became more alert. Was he one of the men who killed the girl?

For several hours, she nursed a man who she hoped was not a terrorist. Now that he has turned out to be a cop, she continues to hope he is not a murderer.

Laila Raza was murdered a few weeks after Akhila's mother died. Even though Akhila was only an adolescent then and current affairs seemed uglier than the story of Mr Mao, she closely followed the noise around Laila's death. As all the people who were accused of killing her were acquitted, some rewarded, and Damodarbhai's stature, in fact, soared, Akhila saw in all that the pointlessness of her mother's indignant life.

Why are the good such duds?

There have been so many heroes who have fought for Laila. There are so many of them even today. They are in the courts pleading with judges who try not to laugh; they are begging for donations to fight the long legal battles; they are debating in television studios in sharp jackets; they are writing essays that are so boring they must be very deep. They are posting on Facebook, too. So many heroes. Yet, they almost always lose. In any other line of work, they would be sacked and replaced by more effective people, but in the battle against villains, the union of dud heroes has ensured for itself an indestructible job security.

SHE THINKS SHE hears his voice. He must have removed his oxygen mask. What can be so important? She is only a few feet away from him but is unable to see his face beyond the beam. She begins to crawl back to reach him, as she cannot turn around. The drill of the approaching second tunnel stops for a few moments and she hears him clearly.

'What's your name?' he asks. His voice is stronger than before but it is still faint.

'Akhila.'

'Akhila.'

'Yes.'

'When I was mumbling things, did I say anything that would get me into trouble?'

'I don't know. You appear to have witnessed an abduction of two people who were eventually killed. I don't know if you were a part of it. I don't know if you are supposed to tell a magistrate or something about what really happened.'

'Anything else?'

'Mukundan, what do you want to know?'

'Nothing.'

'Tell me. I am the person who saved you.'

'Are you a cop?'

'No.'

'Are you a soldier?'

'No. I am a doctor.'

'Akhila.'

'Yes.'

'Did I tell you anything about someone recording phone conversations?'

'No.'

'Those cops outside, do you tell them everything I say?'

'I don't have to.'

'You can if you want to.'

'I know but I don't have to. Do you wish to tell me something?'

He falls silent.

MUKUNDAN FEELS AN irresistible urge to laugh. It must be the fresh air in his lungs, or it could be something else.

HE BEGAN THE recordings the day he learnt about the murders. He recorded all the phone conversations and all his meetings with the Beards.

Nobody took him seriously, nobody saw him for what he was. He began to accumulate a lot of material. He got the phone records of Bhim, which led to the phone records of Black Beard, who is often the voice and the ears of Damodarbhai. During the captivity of Laila Raza, there were fourteen calls between them. There were calls between them just before she was shot and minutes later. Mukundan also taped his conversations with all the Beards who had opened fire. He has hundreds of hours of video and audio records.

Over the years, the Beards began to draw him into their huddles. And he recorded everything. The Beards were taping, too, chiefly their conversations with their seniors and meetings with Black Beard. They did this as leverage to save their asses if some mentally imbalanced judge went after them. They were building evidence that would prove they were only following instructions. Mukundan hunts for this stash, which is stored in phones and even CDs, actually even floppy discs.

People are careful about money, but not about information. That is because they have always gone in pursuit of money and not information. So they keep money in the vault and leave information on the table. If he had set out to steal money, it would have been very difficult. But it is easier to steal the real treasure of people.

He has with him conversations and phone records that implicate Black Beard and the Beard Squad in six sets of murders involving thirteen people. He also has extensive information on the wealth of the Beards.

And he waits. For the Beards to be taken to justice, first Damodarbhai has to fall. That is what the intellectuals do not understand.

Over the decade since the murder of Laila, Damodarbhai has been rising, and he has risen to the level of a minor god. He cannot be destroyed until people fall out of love with him, tire of him, hate him. And one day when they abandon him and he begins to decay, and his rivals in the Sangh come to give him one final blow, only then will he lose the power to guard the Beards. To go to war with him when he is at his peak is to go to war against a sacred hologram beamed by the people.

AFTER HE GETS out of the hole, Mukundan will know how much he has blurted out in his dying slumber. The Beards will be wary of him as they would be of a fragile man with a conscience who knows a bit too much about them. But he might be able to win their trust again. It is a relief that even in his delirium he did not say anything about his decade-long sting on the Squad.

AKHILA RESUMES HER crawl to fresh air, but she stops when she hears him again.

'Akhila.'

'I am here.'

'Who won?'

'Won what?'

'The elections.'

'Damodarbhai.'

'He is my god.'

'Right. Mine too.'

MUKUNDAN WILL WAIT another five years. Then another five, if he has to. But a day will come when Damodarbhai will lose an election. And Mukundan will go to slay the Beards.

He imagines the faces of the Beards when they figure out that they have been done, and a funny thought occurs to him.

THERE ARE FACES only an Indian can make. Like that baffled face when he is shocked by the most logical outcome of his actions. He crosses the road like a cow, and he is startled by a truck. A vehicle on the road? How? He walks across the railway track, and he finds a train hurtling towards him. A train on a railway track? He is stunned. Cops who don't wear bulletproof vests break into a house to fight militants, and they are shot in their paunches. They stagger out looking bewildered. That baffled face, when boys fall off trains because they were dangling from the doorways, when illegal homes built on infirm soil collapse, when pilgrims are squashed in annual stampedes inside narrow temples.

But then the foes of the republic, too, find the face. Sooner or later they all do. Enemies of humanity, criminals, psychotics, all of them. The republic is a giant prank. It lures all into believing that they can do anything and get away with it. And they do get away with a lot. But then one day, inevitably, surprise.

Mukundan is unable to hold it back any more even though it is going to hurt his back.

AKHILA, CRAWLING TOWARDS respite, hears a faint melodious laughter fill the tunnel.

MORE FROM MYRIAD

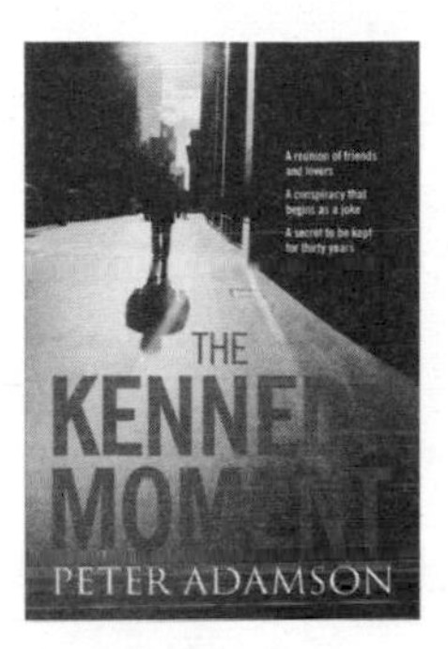

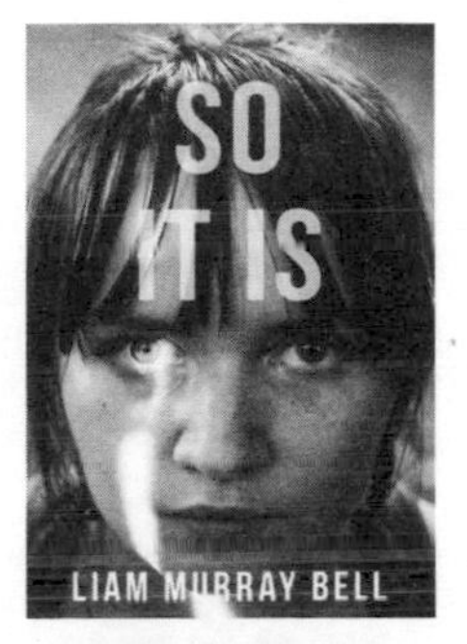

WE GO AROUND IN THE NIGHT AND ARE CONSUMED BY FIRE
JULES GRANT
A story of love, honour and vengeance on Manchester's mean streets

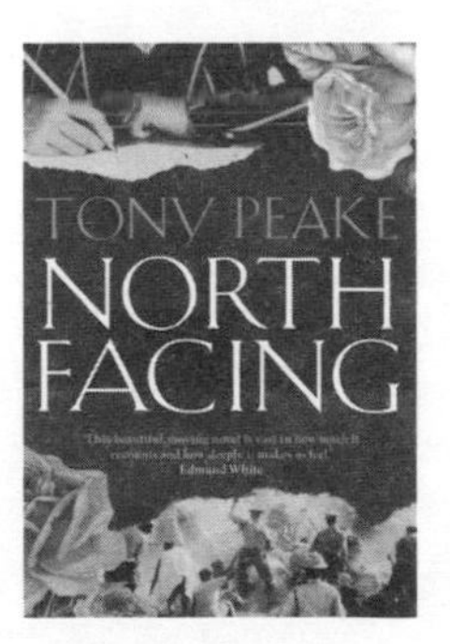

A NOVEL
An English Guide to Birdwatching
Nicholas Royle

myriad